Double Dare of the Gooblyglop

by
Tova Guttmann

Illustrations by
Celia Yitzchak

PITSPOPANY

St. Helier, Jersey

The characters and events in this book
are totally fictitious.

Copyright © 1994
Pitspopany Press and Tova Guttmann

ISBN #9-654-83003-5

Printed in Israel

TABLE OF CONTENTS

CHAPTER ONE
Trust Me

"It's not going to work," declared Sammy.

"Sh-sh-sh," Jonathan whispered without breaking his concentration. "And quit leaning over my shoulder. You're making me nervous."

"You're nuts, Jonathan." Sammy settled himself onto the basement floor. "We've been working on this for months. We have to make our science presentation tomorrow, and it's *never* going to work. I think that we should just use the laser, and forget the other shtick. At least we won't fail. We — "

"HONOLULU! IT'S FINISHED!" Jonathan shouted.

"We finished?"

"Yeah, *we* finished. I finished working and you finished yakking my ears off!" Jonathan got up and stretched his cramped limbs.

"Hey! That's not true! I also...."

"I know, only kidding. But it's done! We're gonna be famous! This is *the* machine that will kill all the mosquitoes in the world! Headlines, Sam. We're gonna make headlines! 'Scientific Whiz Kids Save Mosquito-Bitten World!'"

"'One million dollars were awarded to Jonathan Fireman and Samuel Davies for their amazing invention,'" Sammy continued in his best broadcast voice.

"Maybe we'll be on CNN!" Sammy pretended that the lights of make-believe cameras were flashing in his eyes. He waved his hands and pushed back against the imaginary crowd. Then, smiling, he accidentally tripped over a jumble of wires and found himself flat on his back.

Jonathan looked down at him. "That was pretty realistic. I can see the headline now. 'Silly Scientist Looks Sillier Than Ever Celebrating Success!'"

"Very funny," grumbled Sammy, rubbing his bruised shoulder.

Jonathan put his hands on his hips and surveyed the basement.

The tall 14-year-old took in the scene as if seeing it for the first time. There were tangled messes of wire, resistors, capacitors, IC chips, scrap whatnot, and miscellaneous tools scattered about.

"Sam, this place is a mess. I'm too tired to

*"This is the machine that will kill all the mosquitoes
in the world!"*

straighten up now. Let's get some sleep, and we'll clean up tomorrow."

"Wait a second," Sammy scrambled to his feet. "We can't go to sleep until we finish writing the report — and we need to do a trial run." Sammy was always the more practical of the two.

"Now? At two o'clock in the morning! We've tested the lasers at least eight times. All I did tonight was adjust the scanner. There's no way it'll go wrong. Let's quickly finish writing up the report and then get some sleep."

"And make fools of ourselves in front of the whole class?" Sam countered.

Jonathan saw he was not going to win. "Fine. We can test it tomorrow, if there's time."

"I'll stay up now and test it, I'm not risking my life. Who knows what Mrs. Hensky will do if something goes wrong."

"Nothing's gonna go wrong — trust me."

"Okay," Sammy said, reluctantly giving in. "I'm only listening to you because I'm too tired to argue. But tomorrow morning we test it, whether there's time or not."

"Have I ever steered you wrong?" Jonathan said, with a smile.

CHAPTER TWO
The Amazing Alarm Clock

"Jonathan, wake up!" whispered Sammy urgently. "We're gonna be late!"

At first Jonathan ignored his friend, then he turned over and said groggily, "It can't be that late, my alarm didn't go off yet." As he spoke, the light in his room turned on and a *Shlock Rock* recording sounded at full blast. Jonathan sat bolt upright just in time to avoid being spritzed by the water gun suspended above his bed. An invisible hand yanked his quilt off of him. As he jumped out of bed, a mechanical voice announced, "You have exactly sixteen minutes to get to synagogue. Hurry up!"

Sammy shook his head as he observed the workings of his friend's amazing alarm clock.

Jonathan bounded out of the room to wash up, then hurriedly got dressed. Sammy was already waiting on his bike when Jonathan slammed his way out of the house and wheeled his own bike from the garage. Down the driveway and for six blocks the boys raced against the nippy October wind. Breathless and with bright red ears the boys dashed into the synagogue — almost on time. They quickly donned their tefillin and began their prayers.

Exhausted from lack of sleep, and worried about their science project, the boys had a hard time keeping their minds on what they were saying. While Sammy made sure to slip in a quick prayer for the success of the project, Jonathan found he was just flipping pages, mumbling. With superhuman effort he managed to concentrate on the Silent Prayer, but breathed a sigh of relief when the service was over.

The boys hurried to their bikes and sped back to Jonathan's house. Breakfast was forgotten as they quickly tested their invention (Sammy insisted) and then nervously loaded the experiment and themselves into the car. Jonathan's mother drove them to school.

"Don't blow up the place," she teased them as she waved goodbye.

Little did she know.

CHAPTER 3
The Zapper

PROJECT:

      Voice-Activated Mosquito
      Scanner and Zapper

SUBMITTED BY:

      Samuel H. Davies
      Jonathan Fireman
      GRADE: 9-B

COMPONENTS:

      Micro-processor unit
      Laser
      Tracking Beam
      Zapping Beam
      Laser Beam Splitter
      Electronic Laser Director
      Tracking Detector

Laser Beam Mirrors
High-Voltage Power Supply
Soundproof Casing

GENERAL DESCRIPTION:
A sophisticated hi-tech system consisting of Laser Scanner which divides entire room into a grid of 1mm x 1mm cells.

The scanner identifies location of mosquito, directs the tracking beams onto target, and triggers the laser beam. Once the flying offender is zapped and the room is mosquito-free, the device shuts off automatically.

Aside from the main laser beam, there are also tracking beams which lock onto the alien object until neutralization.

THESE LASERS CANNOT HARM PEOPLE

SETUP:
The laser DDD (director/tracking detector devices) can be placed anywhere in the room. The micro-computer unit will determine fixed coordinates for those units. To initiate operation, push the SETUP button and after 3 seconds the green LED light on the scanner will start blinking, indicating the READY state. The system is now ready for voice activation, which in this instance is the word "Mosquito".

Mrs. Hensky put down the project book and looked over her glasses at the class. The boys shifted uncomfortably under her scrutiny and eventually quieted down.

Mrs. Hensky's eyes made a circuit of the whole lab, taking in the neat rows of equipment that lined the counters of the room. Each work station had its own bunsen burner, microscope, and test-tube holder filled with several test-tubes. Glass slides containing assorted cell slices, blood samples, and insect specimens were neatly displayed everywhere. Visible through glass doors were rows of empty beakers and dozens of bottles containing preserved rodents, crustaceans, and chemicals.

This was the room where Mrs. Hensky felt most at home — the place where she trained students to understand science. Mrs. Hensky tended to be a little over-protective of *her* lab, and didn't allow anyone to tamper with the equipment without her specific direction. She was more than a little concerned about giving her two most imaginative students free rein in her precious lab. But she was determined to suppress her fears, and allow the boys to demonstrate their experiment in class.

After all, thought Mrs. Hensky, as long as I'm in the lab there's little harm they can do. Mrs. Hensky interrupted her thoughts, returning her full attention to the class.

"Gentlemen," she began. "I have here a very impressive-looking report, submitted by Mr. Davies and Mr. Fireman. I would appreciate your undivided attention as they demonstrate their experiment for us."

Jonathan and Sammy made their way to the front of the room. Sammy clutched his notes.

"Okay, Dr. Frankenstein. Go for it!" Bobby whispered.

Howard didn't even bother whispering. "Hey, Jonathan! Where are the pygmy astronauts you promised us? Aren't you launching a satellite?"

"Say what you want," Jonathan shot back. "You're just worried we're gonna get a better grade than you."

"What we're worried about," Michael called out, "is that you're going to turn us all purple, or shrink us to insect size."

Jonathan narrowed his eyes. "Maybe I will," he hissed.

Michael suddenly looked a little nervous.

"Gentlemen!" called Mrs. Hensky as she walked to her vantage point near the back of the room and sat down. "Save your comments until after the demonstration. Then you will be allowed to comment or criticize." She turned to the two budding scientists standing at the front of the room and nodded. "Go ahead."

The Zapper stood silently on the teacher's desk. It looked like a miniature weather station. Even with all its lights and buttons, the Zapper didn't seem capable of producing the correct time, let alone laser rays. One look at it was enough to assure anyone that it was the brainchild of a junk kleptomaniac. The main body of the machine was a discarded metal file-cabinet drawer, the cover had originally been a toaster-oven door, and wires of all sorts and colors were poking out from its sides. There were various sized glass amplifying tubes that Jonathan had salvaged from old TVs. A bicycle inner tube served as the insulator for the high-voltage wires. A discarded carburetor was attached to the machine by a long piece of garden hose. Colored switches and bulbs adorned the outside of the box. In short, the Zapper looked like the leftovers of a dozen different science projects — all unsuccessful!

Jonathan gave his invention a final check while Sammy shuffled his papers nervously.

Finally, Sammy cleared his throat.

"Jonathan and I have prepared a Voice-Activated Mosquito Scanner and Zapper. We believe that this experiment, which we've labored over with much dedication, will prove to be a tremendous success. We are sure that society at large will benefit from this amazing invention.

"As you all know, mosquitoes suck your blood

and annoy you most when you are trying to sleep. During peak mosquito season it is sometimes impossible to ignore them." Looking up from his notes, Sammy realized that he had everybody's full attention. He began to enjoy his role, and continued without reading from his notes.

"So, we've devised a system, using all the latest technology, including lasers, beam-splitters and computer micro-processing units. We aim to rid society of these blood-sucking menaces. Though our ultra complex Scanner-Zapper, which is voice-activated, took hours and hours of in-depth research and assembly by both myself and my associate — "

"Sam," Jonathan hissed. "Quit hamming it up and say what you're supposed to be saying."

"Right, sorry." Everybody laughed. Sammy shuffled his notes again. "As I was saying — when everything is ready, you push the SETUP button — please push it Jonathan, thank you — and as you see, the READY light goes on. You will note there is nothing to spray, no odors or pollutants associated with our machine. In order to destroy the flying offenders you simply shout out the word 'mosquito' and the scanners activate."

"That's dumb," Joey shouted. "Why would anyone want to yell at a machine?"

"But that's exactly the point." Jonathan interrupted. "We don't want the machine going off every time someone speaks. Yelling gives us control over the machine. It activates the Zapper only when we want it to begin operating."

"Anyway," Sammy added, "for today's experiment we raised the voice activator to its highest setting so there could be class participation."

"Class participation?" Mrs. Hensky warily inquired. She was starting to have a funny feeling about the experiment.

"Trust me," Jonathan assured her. "Normally the voice of one person shouting 'mosquito' would be enough to activate the machine. But we thought it would be more interesting if, for this experiment, it were activated when *everyone* in class shouts at the same time."

Mrs. Hensky was debating whether to let the boys continue. But before she could make up her mind Sammy produced a jar.

"We've brought along a mosquito," Sammy began, showing everyone the jar, "which we will now release. When it begins to fly, we ask that *together* everyone shout 'mosquito'. Got it?"

The students nodded.

Jonathan ceremoniously raised the jar to eye level. He began to turn the lid. The silence was hypnotic as everyone stared at the jar, mesmerized. Jonathan finally removed the cover, and placed both jar and lid on the table.

They waited.

And waited.

Sammy and Jonathan peered into the jar, tapped it once, then again, and then looked at each other.

"Is there a problem?" asked Mrs. Hensky.

"It's dead." Sammy whispered.

The class erupted in laughter.

"Way to go, Fireman. You sure put that mosquito out!"

"Yeah, why don't you give it the old *Fireman* carry!"

Sammy looked like he was going to cry.

"WAIT! WAIT!" Jonathan shouted. "It'll work! Watch!"

Jonathan tilted the jar and slid the mosquito onto the palm of his hand. Then he pulled a thread from the bottom of his pants and proceeded to tie it around the insect. "Give me a hand, Sammy," he snapped at his comatose partner.

"What are you gonna do, Jonathan?" Michael called out. "Take your pet mosquito for a walk?"

"No, he's going to hang it, to make sure it's dead!" Howard teased.

"Why don't you give it CPR?" yelled Jeremy.

Ignoring his classmates, Jonathan jumped onto one of the lab tables and reached up to attach the string to a light fixture. As he worked, he spoke above the boys' comments.

"See, it should work anyway — whether the

mosquito is alive or dead. The laser is looking for a mosquito. Any mosquito. When it's alive and flying the Zapper has to calculate its speed and direction before zapping it. Now it will zap the mosquito as soon as the beams triangulate."

There was a gnawing feeling in Mrs. Hensky's stomach. Her instinct was to stop the experiment at this point, but she didn't want to embarrass the boys. They had worked hard and were very determined. Anyway, she told herself, how much damage could a dead mosquito cause?

Jonathan jumped down from the table. The lifeless mosquito hung limply from the fixture.

Sammy finally snapped back into action. "Okay guys, are you ready?"

"All right, everyone," Bobby yelled out, "when he gives the word let's all say Kaddish for the mosquito!"

"Dearly beloved," intoned Jeremy, "we have gathered here today to bid our final farewell to poor, departed, Murray the Mosquito."

Above the noise of his classmates, Sammy began to count. "ONE, TWO..."

"Wait a minute!" Mrs. Hensky called. But it was too late.

"...THREE!"

"M O S Q U I T O!!" shouted 29 voices.

Two beams began probing the room. The students watched, open-mouthed, as a laser suddenly shot out from the box on the teacher's desk and...ZAP!

"Hey! The mosquito is gone!" exclaimed an unbelieving Howard. The class stared at the empty noose hanging from the light fixture. Even Mrs. Hensky looked impressed.

"Well, well," she muttered. "That was quite a demonstration."

Then, eyeing the troublemakers in the class, she said, "I think we all owe Mr. Davies and Mr. Fireman an apology, and I owe you both an A+ for effort and for originality. In fact," Mrs. Hensky paused, "if I find everything in order in your written report, I will be happy to submit your names for the State Junior Science Fair in March."

Jonathan and Sammy were busy doing a little victory dance in front of the room, when one of the beams began probing the room again.

Everyone froze.

CHAPTER 4
She Killed It!

"There must be another mosquito in the room," Sammy announced.

ZAP!

The slide containing the tsetse fly sample in the glass cabinet was suddenly empty.

ZAP! ZAP! ZAP!

Mrs. Hensky jumped up. "Oh no! Turn it off!"

Three more slides were robbed of their specimens.

"Oh no!" echoed the class as they raced for cover.

"Down everyone! Get down!" someone shouted. The boys fought for space under the lab tables.

Near Howard's elbow was a peach pit with a

fruit fly perched on it.

ZAP!

"Yow! We're gonna die in here!" he cried.

"Get me out of here!" shouted Jeremy.

Two boys — covering their heads with their arms and their books — made a dash for the door.

ZAP! ZAP!

The machine continued its work.

A few more boys began crawling toward the door, but the Zapper was scanning the door and the cabinet again.

ZAP! ZAP!

More test slides became empty pieces of glass.

"Mr. Fireman! Turn it off!" Mrs. Hensky shouted above the din.

"I can't!" Jonathan called back. "The scanners automatically turn off on their own when they're finished! I forgot to attach a manual override button!"

ZAP!

Jonathan jumped onto a chair. "Calm down!" he shouted. "The lasers can't hurt you. They're too weak. Trust me!"

ZAP! ZAP! ZAP!

"Crazy, Jonathan — you're crazy!" someone shouted.

BANG! Danny tripped over the trash can as he tried to rush out. His body became wedged between the door and the chairs the students had piled up for cover against the laser rays. The doorway was now blocked.

ZAP! ZAP! ZAP! ZAP!

Boys started jumping out of the ground-floor window.

Mrs. Hensky tried to cover the glass specimen case with her body. But even her ample figure couldn't cover the entire area, and the lasers continued probing the cabinet.

ZAP! ZAP! ZAP! ZAP! ZAP! ZAP!

"TURN IT OFF!" hollered Mrs. Hensky.

Sammy tried to approach the machine, then backed off when it continued zapping. He knew it couldn't hurt him, but it *looked* dangerous.

ZAP! ZAP!

Mrs. Hensky suddenly remembered the new set of slides she had been preparing on her desk. She turned and rushed toward the front of the room.

ZAP! ZAP! ZAP! ZAP! ZAP!

The set of five rare African pygmy flies disappeared.

"Mr. Fireman!" roared Mrs. Hensky, holding up the empty slides. "This set cost over two hundred dollars!"

But Jonathan couldn't hear her over the bedlam.

ZAP! ZAP! ZAP!

A look of hysteria spread across the teacher's

face. Her lab was being destroyed! Overturned furniture, books and papers were scattered everywhere. All those valuable slides, and the expensive equipment she had pleaded and begged the administration to let her buy!

Destroyed.

Zapped.

ZAP! ZAP! ZAP! ·

A crazed Mrs. Hensky suddenly grabbed a chair and threw it at the Zapper! A chair leg caught the edge of the machine and spun it around. The Zapper stopped at the corner of the desk but continued zapping.

The chair flew over the table and landed on a box of new test-tubes. CRASH!

ZAP! ZAP!

Mrs. Hensky took hold of another chair and aimed.

"NO! NO!" shouted Jonathan. You'll ruin it!"

Simultaneously, Sammy and Jonathan lunged toward Mrs. Hensky. As she let the chair fly, they grabbed it and fell to the ground. While they struggled to their feet, the last of their classmates fled the lab. They watched helplessly as Mrs. Hensky charged her desk and jumped onto it. She tried to kick the heavy box, but it wouldn't budge.

ZAP! ZAP!

Jonathan and Sammy watched frozen in disbelief, as Mrs. Hensky sat down on her desk, placed both feet against the machine and shoved it onto the floor!

BANG!!!

Dzzap. Dzippp. The Zapper skittered around wildly for a few seconds, then lay still.

The boys ran over to where their machine lay and looked down at it.

"She killed it!" Sammy gasped.

Jonathan looked on, numbly.

In the distance, ambulance sirens began to wail.

*They watched helplessly as Mrs. Hensky charged her desk
and jumped onto it.*

CHAPTER 5

Purple Walkman

"Here," Jonathan handed Sammy a box as they entered his house. "Dump everything in my room. I'll get us some drinks and something to eat."

Sammy was totally dejected and it was written all over his face. Jonathan, on the other hand, had a spring to his step and was humming to himself.

Sammy sprawled on the bed and stared out the window, miserable. Jonathan returned with two bottles of Coke and some nosh. He took a sip of his drink and opened the box of equipment Sammy had dumped in the corner. He began to absent-mindedly whistle a tune through the gap between his front teeth.

Then, without saying anything, Jonathan left the room only to return a few moments later with a box of spare TV parts and several other gadgets. Whistling all the while, he began to reconstruct the damaged Zapper. Soon he had cleared the broken glass and was re-attaching tubes and wires. When he finished with the internal damage, he proceeded to replace the smashed bulbs from atop the box.

The toaster-oven door that had served as a cover had been totally destroyed. Jonathan went to his closet and rummaged around until he came up with a rectangular aluminum Hanukkah Menorah. Last year his little brother, Jeremy, had decided to clean the Menorah with some steel wool and had worn away all the candle holders. Only the cheap aluminum frame remained.

"I knew I'd find a use for this," Jonathan said aloud, as he flattened the aluminum into a cover. He wiped his hands from the oily residue that covered the Menorah, reminiscent of the olive oil his father always used on Hanukkah.

"Is there anything you *do* throw away?" Sammy asked watching his pal putter around with what was left of their mosquito-scanning equipment.

Suddenly, there was a loud noise at the door, and Jonathan's 10-year-old sister stormed in. She stood in the middle of the room with her arms folded and glared at her brother.

"Okay, where is it?" demanded Tami.

"Hi! Nice to see you, too," said Jonathan.

"Don't give me that," Tami continued hotly. "What did you do with it?"

"I ate *it*, okay?" Jonathan said, staring at his sister. "I couldn't help myself. I saw whatever *it* is and I just gobbled *it* up. Oh yes, *it* pleaded with me, 'Please don't eat me, please don't eat me,' *it* said but I ate *it* anyway. Satisfied?"

Sammy couldn't repress a grin. Even Tami seemed on the verge of a smile. Then she realized her brother was pulling her leg.

"You're not funny!" Tami cried, looking from Jonathan to Sammy, who was trying hard to control his laughter. "Where is my purple Walkman? I know you took it for one of your Frankenstein experiments. What did you do with it? Why can't you leave my things —"

"Listen here, Madame Dope," Jonathan interrupted, tired of her nagging. "In case your brain leaked out of your ears, I'll remind you that your purple Walkman has been broken for about four months. You hardly used it anyway — why are you looking for it now?"

"None of your business, Mr. Nosey," Tami shot back. "All I know is that it disappeared and when things suddenly disappear around here, *I* know who takes them."

"How can you use it, if it doesn't work?" Jonathan asked, honestly curious.

"I wear it in school because Tanya has the same one and that way we match!" Tami explained.

"But it doesn't work!" Jonathan said, missing the point. Then he realized what she was saying. "You mean to tell me that you wear a broken purple Walkman just to *match* your best friend? Are you normal?" Jonathan clearly didn't understand 10-year-old girls at all.

"Give it back! I know you have it!" Tami insisted, looking around the room.

Sammy stopped laughing and started feeling uncomfortable. He knew, as did Jonathan, that the Walkman no longer existed. A few days ago they had *borrowed* the broken Walkman for its miniature parts. "Well, I sort of don't have it," Jonathan admitted.

Tami's eyes narrowed. "What do you mean 'sort of'? What did you do with it?"

"Nothing terrible, don't worry. I just —" Jonathan paused, searching for a safe word. "I, um, I embalmed it."

Sammy stifled another laugh.

"What does that mean?" asked Tami suspiciously.

"Nothing terrible. Listen, you don't care that it doesn't work, right? I'll have it ready for you in a few hours. Trust me — you'll match Tanya tomorrow."

"You'd better unbalm it, or whatever you did

to it!" Tami fumed. "And keep out of my room from now on! Leave all my things alone or I'll start balming some of your things too!"

Tami stalked out of the room and slammed the door.

Jonathan looked at Sammy.

"Embalmed it, huh?" Sammy chuckled. "You better make sure she doesn't tell your mummy!" he laughed, pleased with his pun.

Jonathan didn't join in the laughter. "I'll just put the outside back together again," he said. "She only needs the empty shell of the Walkman in order to *match*." Jonathan shook his head, and returned to repairing the Zapper.

"I wonder if I can get this thing to zap weird little sisters," he mumbled to himself.

CHAPTER 6
Meet Gooblyglop

Three days later, Sammy looked on as Jonathan put the finishing touches on the Zapper. He bent the Hanukkah Menorah into place. "Why are you fixing it again?" Sammy asked.

"Y'know, Sammy," Jonathan said without looking up, "You shouldn't have gotten so worked up about this. It was hardly broken. I've basically fixed it already."

"Jonathan, are you CRAZY?!" Sammy began to pace the room and wave his hands around as he spoke. "You put it back together? After what happened at school? What's the matter with you?"

"Nothing's the matter with me," declared Jonathan. "I just want to set up the Zapper so I won't have mosquitoes in my room any more. I'll sleep better at night."

"You may sleep better, but there are lots of people in this town who are going to be very angry when your Zapper finishes zapping every flying thing within a hundred miles of here! I can see all the empty bird cages now!"

"Cut it out, Sam. The Zapper is too weak to zap anything but teeny tiny mosquitoes...and maybe some small specimens that Mrs. Hensky kept around. Now let me finish this." Jonathan continued his work. "Anyway, you know as well as I do that the experiment was a real success. So what if Mrs. H. freaked out — that's not the end of the world! Maybe she just needs a vacation! The Zapper is still a great invention — I'm not going to ditch the whole thing just because of one minor mistake."

"A *minor* mistake? You call forgetting to put in a stop button a *minor* mistake!?"Sammy spluttered. "I'd love to know what you call a *major* mistake. In case you've forgotten, let me review some of the results of your *minor* mistake: Mark sprained his ankle, Howard probably fractured his collarbone, Joey has a black eye, and David, well, David is still in the hospital under observation. I spoke to his brother and he said that once they figure out why David keeps ducking every time someone turns on a light, they'll be able to release him. I think the Gulf War had less casualties than our so-called 'successful experiment'.

"Oh yes, and let's not forget all the one-of-a-kind insect slides we'll probably have to pay for for the rest of our lives. And then, of course, there's our principal, who, if you remember, has threatened to have us expelled not only from our school but from every school in North America if we ever even think of doing our experiment again. You don't want to finish high school in Mexico, do you? Let's see, have I forgotten anyone? Oh yes, I have, haven't I. Mrs. Hensky. The little old psychotic science teacher they carried away cursing you, me and the Zapper. You realize, of course, that we still have to face her for three more years. And to think, I once even had thoughts of becoming a doctor. Do you think they accept students in medical school with an overall grade of F in science? Hey! But if you think we were a success, I certainly don't want to rain on your parade.... Dummy!"

Jonathan shrugged his shoulders, smiled, and continued his work. "That's quite a speech," he told his friend. "Maybe you should join the debating team? Anyway, I still say it was a success. It zapped the mosquito, didn't it? It scanned and found other flying insects too. That's what it was supposed to do, and it did! By *my* terms, I call that a success."

"So you think if you put it back together it

won't kill anyone?"

"Maybe just wing 'em," Jonathan answered sarcastically. He straightened up and brushed off his hands. "Finished."

"What?"

"Yeah. It should work fine now."

Sammy went to get his backpack. "If you're going to activate that thing again, I'm leaving! I'm too young to die!"

Jonathan pushed the SETUP button, and the READY light went on.

Sammy ran for the door, but before he could reach it he heard the ominous word —

"MOSQUITO!"

A laser began scanning the bedroom.

"You dweeb!" said Sammy, under his breath.

He stood there with his backpack slung over his shoulder. The beams played on his face and clothing and then continued their search. Suddenly, a look of realization spread across Sammy's face. Jonathan was right. It *was* a success! Just look at how systematically and gracefully the lasers were scanning the room! Sammy dropped his pack to the floor and the two partners stood silently enjoying the light show.

And then it happened.

As the probing beam swept past Jonathan's desk the laser suddenly erupted into a prism of colors! Sparks appeared to be shooting out in all directions! Jonathan and Sammy dove for cover as a shimmering light engulfed the room.

After about a minute, Jonathan peered out from under his quilt.

"Sammy?"

"Yeah?" came the muffled reply.

"Where are you?"

"Under the bed."

"Take a look at that!"

Floating in the middle of Jonathan Fireman's bedroom was a multi-colored, 3-dimensional image. As it rotated, letters began to float around the room. It looked as if a message were being written in mid-air.

"What did you do?" Sammy whispered.

"I-I-I don't know," Jonathan stammered. "I just stuck in some spare pieces to fix it. It shouldn't be any different than it was before."

"You dummy!" Sammy scolded. "You intercepted somebody's fax machine!"

Jonathan shot Sammy a sideways glance. "That's not how faxes work, dodo."

"So what is it?"

As the boys looked on, the shimmering image began to solidify.

"It looks like words!" Jonathan exclaimed.

"I think they spell 'You're dead'," moaned Sammy.

Jonathan hit Sammy over the head with a pil-

Jonathan and Sammy dove for cover as a shimmering light
engulfed the room.

low. "Stop being a wimp!"

The colors shattered when the pillow passed through the image. The boys dove for cover a second time, then looked out to see the letters re-solidify in the center of the glimmering haze.

Sammy found his voice. "What's it saying? All I see are letters floating around."

Jonathan moved to the corner of the room. "This is really amazing, Sammy. Whatever angle you look at the letters from, they look like they're facing you. It's a hologram! I must've invented a holographic communications system!" Jonathan became very excited. "I've discovered a new means of communication! It'll replace telephones! WOW! NASA's going to want to know about this! Maybe they'll ask me to work for them, or give me a scholarship to M.I.T. Or maybe they'll offer me — "

"This is NUTS!" Sammy exploded. "Is this another one of your wacky experiments?"

"Wacky? This is more than wacky. This is genius! Let's see what we can do with this thing. We may have a real scientific revolution on our hands!" Jonathan's enthusiasm couldn't be dampened.

"You know what I think?" Sammy sounded nervous. "I think you've intercepted a coded message. For all you know, the FBI or CIA are closing in on us now. Turn the stupid thing off!"

"No way, Sammy. I want to see what will happen."

One by one, the letters hovering above them began to move toward the center of the hazy cloud and vanish into an invisible hole.

"We're missing the message! Get a pen!" Jonathan ran to his knapsack and rummaged around for a pen.

As letters were swallowed up the haze gathered into itself, fading into a pinpoint, like an old-fashioned TV set being turned off.

"Oh! We missed it!" Jonathan slammed the desk. When he looked down where his hands rested he suddenly noticed that there was something written on the blank piece of paper that had been left there. The letters were transparent and colorless, as if they had been written with water. He could just make out the faintest image.

"Hey, Sammy! Look at this!" he yelled, excitedly.

Sammy hurried over to the desk, and as the laser beams continued probing the room, the two boys studied the message on the paper.

Sammy called off the letter. "N C G G N G L K Y R M C H N." Jonathan looked at Sammy. "What do you make of that?"

Sammy looked at the paper, and shrugged. "Gooblyglop."

"What?"

"I said, gooblyglop."

"I heard what you said. What do you mean by

that?"

"I mean it makes no sense. There's not one vowel in the whole message. It's plain gooblyglop."

"Maybe it really is a secret message, like you said before," Jonathan suggested. "Maybe if we substitute —"

Before Jonathan could continue, the probing beam swept past the desk and once again the room was enveloped in a 3-dimensional colorful haze with letters swirling in its midst.

"Put another blank paper on the desk," Sammy suggested.

"Wait, I have a better idea." Jonathan turned on his computer and printer. Once again letters swirled around in mid-air in a seemingly senseless order and then began disappearing into a tiny black hole at the center of the haze.

When the haze had entirely disappeared, Jonathan and Sammy turned to the computer. Complete words were being printed.

Sammy read the message aloud.

> THANK YOU
> YOUR MACHINE MAKES IT EASIER
> SORRY ABOUT THE VOWELS
> FORGOT ABOUT THOSE
> WHAT I SAID BEFORE WAS
> NICE GGOING I LIKE YOUR MACHINE

Both boys were silent for a minute.

Sammy found his voice first. "This is freaky," he observed.

"Not freaky..." Jonathan slowly exclaimed, "Awesome! This is either a voice-activated-direct-dial-paperless fax machine, or else..."

"Or else what?" Sammy challenged.

"Or an alien." Jonathan faced the center of his room and raised his voice. "Who are you?" He asked.

The laser beam momentarily shattered again, and then solidified. The printer suddenly sprang to life.

"GGOOBLYGLOP" Jonathan read out loud.

Sammy's eyebrows shot up. "Gooblyglop? B-but tha-that's what I said you were!"

Following another alphabet-swirling sequence, a new message appeared.

> *RIGHT*
>
> *YOU SAID I'M GGOOBLYGLOP*
>
> *I LIKE THAT NAME*

"I meant..." Sammy began. "Oh, forget it."

Jonathan laughed. Okay, Gooblyglop. Nice to meet you. I hope you don't mind if we call you Goobie." Jonathan spoke to the center of his room. "Where are you? What kind of machine are you speaking through?"

When Gooblyglop didn't answer, Jonathan said, "Goobie, are you still there?"

A few seconds later a message appeared.

I AM NOT THERE JONATHAN

I AM HERE

"Hey, it knows my name!" Jonathan exclaimed.

"You know what," Sammy suddenly said, "I'm beginning to think we're on Candid Camera or something. Is this really happening?"

Jonathan laughed. "Who cares! Let's ask it more questions." Once again, Jonathan projected his voice to the middle of his bedroom.

"Why have you contacted us?"

Sammy started to mimic his friend. "Woooo! Earth base to Venus. Earth base to Venus! Come in Venus."

"Why did you contact us?" Jonathan repeated, choosing to ignore Sammy's sound effects and childish comments.

But Sammy wasn't finished yet.

"Uh, I'm sorry," he said, with a high-pitched Midwestern accent, "the alien you have called is not in service. Please deposit your left ear and dial again."

He started to laugh but stopped short as words began to appear and the printer started working.

GGOOBIE DARES YOU

TO DO ALL I SAY

EVERY LITTLE DETAIL

IN GGOOBIE'S SPECIAL WAY

CHAPTER 7
Dare #1

"I don't believe this! This is *great*" Jonathan exclaimed. "Our own private alien!"

"But, why?" Sammy questioned the haze. "Why do you want to dare us?"

A million letters exploded, forming the words:

DARE TO SAVE HUMANS

"Hey," Sammy wondered out loud, "is this guy for real?"

The letters suddenly shifted and changed.

NOT GGUY

GGOOBIE

"What are you talking about?" Sammy demanded.

TRUST ME

"That's what Jonathan says just before he destroys my sanity," Sammy muttered.

"Let's go for it!" said Jonathan enthusiastically.

"Jonathan," Sammy whispered, certain that the alien could not hear. "Don't you think we should tell someone about this, I mean a parent, or the government? Who knows what this thing really wants?"

Again the same words:

TRUST ME

"So much for keeping a secret from this thing," Sammy said out loud. "Okay, count me in," Sammy finally agreed, although much less excited than his friend. "But this better not be too dangerous," he warned.

NOT TOO DANGEROUS

VERY IMPORTANT

Now the letters began to appear faster. Too fast for the boys to read in the air. The printer exploded, racing at 300 letters a minute.

Finally, the printer stopped. Jonathan picked up the paper. There was a full page of very clear instructions. Jonathan read them aloud:

THESE THINGS YOU MUST DO AT ONCE

DON'T DELAY

DO THEM NOW EXACTLY AS I SAY

Sammy groaned. "I just *know* we're in for it."

1. FIRST GGO GGET ELASTIC

JUMP ROPE

FROM ROOM OF GGIRL WHOSE

NAME IS MADAME DOPE

Both boys started to laugh. Her name is really Tami," Sammy called out to Goobie. "Jonathan just calls her Madame Dope."

"And that's one of the nicer things I call her," Jonathan added, and then continued to read aloud.

> 2. *TIE ROPE TO OPPOSITE WALLS*
> *LET ENDS HANG*
> *STRETCH IT WELL SO IT IS TIGHT*
> *AS CAN BE*
> *2 FEET FROM THE CEILING*
> *MAXIMUM 3*

"Well, at least it stopped rhyming," interjected Sammy. "Sort of. I never did like poetry," he said to the floating letters.

> 3. *PLACE ZAPPER MACHINE NEAR ONE*
> *OF THE WALLS*
> *TIE END OF ROPE TO RED KNOB*
> 4. *HANG MICROWAVE FROM CENTER*
> *OF ROPE*
> *DON'T LET IT FALL*
> *FALL AND YOU FAIL*

"Fall and I die," Jonathan corrected. "We just got the microwave back from the repair shop yesterday — again. Mom blames me for all the electrical failures around here. If something happens to the microwave she'll put me up for adoption, or donate me to Mrs. Hensky for her experiments. Goobie, are you sure we need to use a microwave?"

Letters whirled and a message appeared

I WILL ADOPT YOU

OR EXPERIMENT

Both boys were silent for a moment. "You don't think he means it, I mean about the experiment," Sammy said.

"Of course not," Jonathan told him, trying to convince himself as well as his friend. "He just repeats things, that's all. I trust him."

"Well, I for one like the idea about adopting you," Sammy admitted, accepting Jonathan's assessment of the situation. "That way you can finally write that book you've always been talking about, *Good Times On The Planet Zargon* or better yet, *My Mom The GGooblyglop*. It'll sell millions!"

Not wanting to encourage Sammy, Jonathan continued reading.

5. PUT ON COATS AND SUNGLASSES

6. STRAP SLEEPING BAGS ACROSS
   YOUR BACKS

7. GGET FLUORESCENT LAMP
   PUT IT ON DESK
   HOOK IT UP TO ZAPPER
   THEN TURN IT ON

8. GGET PIANO BENCH
   CLIMB ON MICROWAVE
   TURN ON ZAPPER AND COUNT TO 70

Jonathan spoke quickly. "I'm not too excited

about this last part. Climbing on a microwave could be hazardous to my health. Especially if the microwave falls."

"Well, bigshot," Sammy teased, "Now that it's getting a little dangerous you're singing another tune."

"Okay, you're right!" Jonathan admitted, "I'm letting my fears get in the way of whatever important mission Goobie has in store for us. And anyway, a dare's a dare. I'm going to see this through."

Jonathan thought for a second.

"You get the piano bench and a lamp. I'll get the jump rope from Tami's room. I just hope she's not around. I'll get the other stuff except the microwave. We'll do that together."

"I'll get our coats, too." Sammy offered.

"Okay, good. But let's hurry."

"What about Goobie?" Sammy asked. "You still going to be here?" he asked the air.

The printer clicked out:

WHEN READY YELL MOSQUITO

CHAPTER 8

Just Hanging Around

All the items Goobie requested lay in a heap in the center of the room. Jonathan and Sammy eased the microwave onto the bed, then looked around.

"This better work fast," Jonathan said. "My mom will be back within the hour. She might get a bit suspicious when she tries to heat up supper and discovers the microwave is gone."

"Let's call Goobie, to make sure we do this right the first time," suggested Sammy.

"MOSQUITO!" yelled the duo.

The lasers began systematically probing the bedroom. Once again the beams seemed to shatter into millions of tiny light particles. The brilliant flash caught the boys off guard momentarily. Then they watched the letters forming the words:

GGOOBIE HERE
GGO

The boys set to work quickly. Jonathan kept glancing at his watch, nervous that they wouldn't finish in time. Twenty minutes later, Tami's elastic jump rope was stretched tight across the room, with one end attached to the knob of the Zapper's scanner. "Give me a hand, Sammy," Jonathan called to his friend. "It needs to be very tight. Hey!" Jonathan suddenly noticed what Sammy was working on. "Where did you take that lamp from?"

"From the basement — I noticed it when we were working down there the other day," Sammy answered, defensively.

"Why couldn't you take the ugly one near the piano, instead?"

"You mean the one your mother loves? Don't you think she'll be a little suspicious when she finds so many things missing in the house? I figured nobody would miss this ugly thing. Besides, that one's not fluorescent."

"Oh! That's true. Only my father's been working on adapting this one. He's raising the frequency so it won't attract bees. I hope he won't notice it's gone."

"We'll put it back before he misses it," Sammy assured his friend. "Trust me," he smiled.

"Okay, okay. You done? Come give me a hand."

The boys arranged everything just as Goobie had directed them. They were particularly careful about the microwave, making sure to strap it very securely. When they finished, the microwave looked like a ski lift suspended in mid-air over the center of the room.

Next, the boys put on the clothes Goobie had instructed them to wear.

"You look like a dork," Jonathan commented after looking his pal over.

"Ditto to you, dweeb."

Both boys were bundled in winter coats and wearing sunglasses, with sleeping bags rolled up and slung across their backs. The fluorescent lamp was switched on creating an eerie glow throughout the room. The piano bench was set up under the microwave.

"Let's do it!" Jonathan said, jumping onto the bench. Sammy took a deep breath, and followed. From his perch, Jonathan steadied the microwave as Sammy climbed onto it. He sat, cowboy style at one end. But when Jonathan tried to mount the microwave, the whole contraption began to sway. "Hey, take it easy!" Sammy yelled. "I feel like I'm riding a bronc!" Jonathan waited until the oven steadied itself, and then tried to climb aboard again. This time, he succeeded in getting halfway up when suddenly the rope began to sag ever so slightly at the center.

"Watch out!" shouted Sammy as he spread out on his stomach hugging the microwave. All at once, the microwave started to rotate. Suddenly, he found himself upside down. "Where are you?" he called out.

Jonathan was busy turning an unexpected somersault in the air. He would have ended up on the floor, if not for the sleeping bag that became hopelessly entangled in the rope. Instead, he found himself suspended upside-down, bouncing slightly with the elasticity of the jump rope.

"Help me, Sammy!" Jonathan shouted.

But Sammy was laughing too hard.

"Hey! Cut it out! It's not funny!" Jonathan struggled to release himself. "Sammy, *do* something!"

Sammy caught his breath. You just hanging around, or are you gonna get on with the program?" he said, and burst into renewed peals of laughter.

Jonathan tried to reach for the rope to regain his balance. Each time he moved, Sammy would start rocking again.

"Stop moving around so much! You're gonna make the whole thing collapse!" Sammy yelled.

"Fine," Jonathan agreed, looking like a fly caught in a spider's web. "But I've got to reach over and pull the end of the rope near the Zapper so the scanner can start. Then I'm gonna count to

"You just hanging around, or are you gonna get on with the program?"

seventy. That should free us from this stupid dare and then we'll get out of this crazy contraption, if I have to rip everything apart myself."

Jonathan leaned over as far as he could and pulled the end of the rope that started the Zapper humming. Rays appeared almost at once. They were very bright, glowing with a vibrancy that made him squint his eyes, even with the sunglasses on.

"Hey, Sammy, we didn't even have to say mosquito," he said.

"As long as it still only *kills* mosquitos, and other flying objects that are not attached to microwaves, I don't care what happens."

Then Jonathan began counting.

He was up to 57 when suddenly the bedroom door flew open. Jonathan's mother stood at the doorway, a look of disbelief in her eyes.

"Uh, hi Mom!" Jonathan smiled craning his neck to get a clear view of his mother.

"WHAT - ON - EARTH - DO - YOU - THINK - YOU'RE - DOING?" Mrs. Fireman shouted at the sight of her son and his friend suspended in midair.

"Uh, I seem to have gotten caught on something," Jonathan answered casually. Under his breath he continued counting. "Fifty-eight, fifty-nine...."

Mrs. Fireman's gaze rested on the suspended

microwave. Sammy tried to smile and wave at the same time, but he almost fell off in the attempt.

"WHAT ARE YOU DOING WITH MY MI-CROWAVE?!?" she shouted.

"Is this yours?" Sammy meekly answered. "I told Jonathan it looked familiar."

"Traitor! Sixty, sixty-one..." Jonathan whispered. Then, trying hard to think of an excuse, he said, "Really, Mom, we didn't ruin it or anything (sixty-two, sixty-three, sixty four...). We were just trying an — "

"DON'T SAY EXPERIMENT! DON'T EVEN THINK IT! YOU'RE GROUNDED FOR A WEEK! FOR A MONTH! NOW GET DOWN!"

"(Sixty-five, sixty-six, sixty-seven...) No, what I meant to say is that (sixty-eight, sixty-nine).... We just... SEVENTY!" Jonathan yelled startling his mother.

Mrs. Fireman was livid. She decided to appeal to the weaker of the two maniacs. "Samuel Davies, you come down from that microwave RIGHT NOW! I'm going to call your mother and have you grounded as well. We *just* got it back from the repair shop, and..."

"Whatever you say, Mrs. Fireman." Sammy let go of the microwave and fell onto the floor with a WHAPP! He immediately unwound himself and helped release his wriggling friend.

"Don't pull too hard," Jonathan whispered to

Sammy. "If the microwave falls I'll be grounded... six feet under!"

"BOTH OF YOU!" Mrs. Fireman commanded the duo, impatiently. "I WANT TO SEE THAT MICROWAVE IN ITS PLACE *AND* PROPERLY ATTACHED IN *FIVE* MINUTES." With that ultimatum delivered, she stalked out.

Sammy gave a final tug and Jonathan was released from the jump rope's clutches. The boys scrambled to take off their winter coats and free the microwave.

"At least we finished the dare," Jonathan said, as they worked. " Did you see how bright the rays were? Something happened all right. I wish I could analyze the Zapper now to see exactly —"

Sammy shook his head. "Sometimes I can't believe you, Jonathan. How can you be thinking about dares and zappers right now?"

"Well, this must all have a purpose right? Wouldn't it be terrible if it accomplished its purpose and we didn't even know it?"

"Jonathan, I think that whatever is suppose to happen hasn't happened yet but when it does we'll notice it. That I'm sure of."

As they gently lowered the microwave to the floor Jonathan suddenly started to smile. "You know what's really funny," he said, "my mother didn't even notice the scanner rays. She was so worried about her microwave she just ignored the rays whizzing by."

"She didn't ignore them," Sammy said. "It's just that she's used to weird things happening in here. She probably thought you have rays floating around here all the time."

They both laughed.

After returning the microwave to its proper place in the kitchen, the boys straightened up Jonathan's bedroom. When they finished, Sammy picked up his knapsack and prepared to leave.

"What a day!" Jonathan commented.

"You said it!" Sammy agreed. "It's just too bad about getting grounded. If your mom keeps you in for more than a week you won't be able to get out for Succot vacation."

"It's okay," Jonathan answered. "I'll have plenty to do at home — my Dad's gonna want my help putting up the Succah anyway. And now with Goobie around, I have a feeling time will fly. I'm only worried about one thing."

"What's that?"

Jonathan held up a limp, overstretched, elastic jump rope.

"Tami's going to KILL me!"

CHAPTER 9
Dare #2

Jonathan peddled his bike furiously, trying to overtake a bus. The bus put on a sudden burst of speed and made it through the intersection just before the light turned red. Jonathan caught a faceful of exhaust. Coughing, he braked quickly and gasped for some clean air.

While he waited for the light to change, Jonathan checked the box that was strapped to the back of his bike. Today, his week of being grounded had ended (his mother had been merciful), and he was on his way over to Sammy's house. The Zapper, of course, accompanied him.

The light turned green, and Jonathan took off again. His nose and ears were bright red from the brisk October air. He bent his head against the cool breeze and tried to peddle faster. He turned down a tree-lined street and rode his bicycle through a pile of brittle, brown leaves. KRUNCH! Jonathan took a deep breath of crisp air, then swung his bike into the dead-end street where Sammy lived.

Out in time for Succot vacation! thought Jonathan joyfully as he swooped into the Davies' driveway. His back wheel suddenly skidded out from under him and he barely managed to prevent the bike from crashing to the ground, Zapper and all.

"Nice save!" called a voice.

Jonathan looked up to see 8-year-old Abie Davies peering down at him from a tree.

"Thanks, Abie." Jonathan smiled up at his friend's impish little brother. "For my next act..."

Abie jumped down from the tree. "What do you have in the box?"

"What do you want it to be?" Jonathan shot back as he wheeled his bike up to the garage. Abie followed behind him.

"A snake!"

"Borrrring. Can't you think of anything a little more exciting?"

"A giant squid!"

"BINGO!" yelled Jonathan.

"Really?" Abie asked excitedly.

"Sure," Jonathan said, thinking for a moment. "It's a S.Q.U.I.D. all right. Super Quiet Insect Destroyer."

"Wow! A destroyer! A-1!" Abie exclaimed.

"What you gonna destroy?" he asked.

Jonathan picked up the heavy box and lugged it towards the back door. "Monster mosquitoes," he yelled over his shoulder as he rang the bell.

"Come on in, Jonathan!" Sammy's mother called.

"Thanks, Mrs. Davies." Jonathan struggled through the door with the large box. "Mmm! It smells great in here," he commented.

"I always bake a lot on Succot," Mrs. Davies said, smiling. "Sammy's setting up for dinner in the Succah. By the way, we haven't seen you around for a while. Where have you been?"

"Been?" Jonathan repeated, realizing that Sammy had neglected to tell his mother about their little adventure. "I've been staying close to home so I could help my mother prepare for Succot."

"That's sweet," Mrs. Davies said. "I wish Sammy was like that."

"No you don't," Jonathan mumbled under his breath.

"What was that, Jonathan?" she asked.

"Donuts," Jonathan answered. "I love your donuts," he said, eyeing the tray she had just taken out of the oven.

"Well, then here's a special one for you," she offered.

"Thanks!" Jonathan grabbed the donut and hurried to find his pal.

In the Succah, Jonathan and Sammy had time to catch up on the past few days' events. Since the day of the science presentation, each boy had been very busy helping his father put up their wooden Succah. It was only now, after the first two days of Succot, that the boys had been able to get together to make vacation plans.

Jonathan sank his teeth into the donut.

"So, what's the urgent thing you came over to tell me?" asked Sammy. "And why couldn't you tell me about it on the phone?"

"Yumph," Jonathan answered through a mouthful of donut. He swallowed. "I couldn't talk because Tami was in the room and she wouldn't leave. She keeps pestering me about her Walkman. She insists it doesn't rattle like it used to. Anyway, it's about Goobie."

Sammy rolled his eyes. "Not again! Listen, if I dared you not to accept another dare would you do it?"

"No. Come on, do you really have something better to do?"

"Actually I do," Sammy answered. "I was hoping to sky dive, bungee jump, and climb Mount Everest. I figure they're all tamer than what that alien has planned for us."

Jonathan shook his head. "Very funny. But wait

until you hear what happened last night. I was so tired that I didn't even bother to activate the scanner before I went to sleep. When I woke up this morning, there was a message anyway! Goobie somehow activated the laser on his own!"

"Great! Maybe we can get him to do the dares on his own too!"

Jonathan pulled a paper from his pocket and unfolded it on the table. "Here's the message."

I'M HERE
YOU HAVE TO GGET MOVING OR YOU'LL
CAUSE GGREAT SORROW
GGOOBIE DARES YOU TO DO THIS
TOMORROW

1. GGO UP ON THE ROOF AND SET UP
   THE ZAPPER
   MAKE SURE IT IS ABOVE THE HEIGHT
   OF YOUR LITTLE HOUSE SUCCAH
   CAREFUL NOW
   BE SURE TO TIE ONE END OF A ROPE
   AROUND YOURSELF AND THE OTHER
   END TO THE CHIMNEY

2. TIE STRINGS TO 4 SPOONS AND FILL
   THEM WITH HONEY
   YOU MUST BRING THE BEES AS FAST
   AS YOU CAN

3. PLACE HANGER AT END OF A
   CURTAIN STICK

4. EAT 20 M&MS

5. HOLD ONTO STICK

*6. PUT THE SPOONS ONTO THE HOOK
   OF THE HANGER SO THEY ARE
   HANGING OVER THE SUCCAH*

*7. WHILE YOU ARE HANGING THERE
   RECITE NATIONAL ANTHEM*

GGOOD LUCK

REMEMBER NOT TOO DANGEROUS

VERY IMPORTANT

"This is ridiculous!" Sammy exclaimed.

"Perhaps," Jonathan retorted. "But who knows? Maybe we're saving the world."

"Talk about delusions of grandeur," Sammy smirked. "And why'd you decide to bring the Zapper here and do the dare at my house? So *I'll* get grounded this time?" he said accusingly.

"That's not why," Jonathan insisted. "It's because our Succah doesn't have any bees. That lamp my father rigged seems to have worked."

He paused. "The problem is that I don't know the National Anthem by heart too well. I do know Hatikvah though."

"Well I know the Anthem but not much of Hatikvah, so we're even," Sammy countered. "You say your anthem and I'll say mine."

"Deal."

The boys cleaned up and went inside the

house.

"You think you could sleep here tonight?" Sammy suggested as they were assembling the things they would need.

"Maybe. I'd have to ask."

"Then ask. I think we should do this at night so I don't get killed for it. Especially if my mother sees we took the shower curtain rod! It's better if we do it after everyone is asleep."

"Good idea!" Jonathan agreed.

A quick phone call and a dash home by bike to get pajamas and a change of clothes was all it took.

"Easy as pie," Jonathan said as he threw his clothes onto Sammy's extra bed. "Let's get the stuff ready for the dare."

Sammy sat at the edge of his bed. "Why don't I feel good about this?" he groaned.

CHAPTER 10
This Is NUTS!

By 11:30 p.m. the whole Davies household was asleep. Sammy and Jonathan donned heavy sweaters against the cold October night air and stealthily made their way to the garage to get the stuff they had prepared.

Together they carried the box to the side of the house. The moon provided enough light for them to make their way easily through the flower bed without using flashlights. Next, Sammy brought the tall ladder from the basement, and leaned it against the house.

"You first, or me?" Jonathan broke the silence.

"Sh-sh-sh," Sammy whispered.

Using hand signals, the boys managed to communicate as they pulled their equipment up the ladder.

Once everything was in order on the roof they got to work attaching the Zapper securely just above the Succah.

They tied long ropes around themselves and fastened the ends to the wide chimney.

"Make sure it's very tight," Jonathan whispered to Sammy.

"You bet," Sammy whispered back .There's a strong wind up here, besides the fact that it's slippery. Let's hurry up!"

Sammy took out a jar of honey from the box. He busied himself tying strings to the four spoons he'd brought along, and then coated them with honey. Meanwhile, Jonathan concentrated on firmly attaching the hanger to the shower curtain rod. He was using scotch tape to hold the hanger in place. Every time he pulled the tape to take another piece a resounding "TSSST" ripped through the night air.

"Can't you keep quiet?" said Sammy in a whisper.

"Let's see *you* tear tape quietly!" Jonathan shot back. He tried instead to pull the tape bit by bit, which proved to be quieter, but much more time-consuming. Sammy began to get more nervous.

"You ready yet?" asked Sammy.

"Yeah," replied Jonathan as he gave a final tug. "Let's get started."

They crawled to the edge of the roof, and Jonathan prepared to lower himself a few feet so he'd be directly above the Succah.

"Wait!" Sammy suddenly whispered. "We forgot the M&Ms!"

Sammy scampered quickly to the box and pulled out a jumbo pack of M&Ms.

"Couldn't you find a smaller bag?" Jonathan asked.

"I grabbed what there was — d'you mind?" Sammy shot back.

The boys quickly counted out 20 M&Ms apiece and gobbled them, shivering in the biting wind.

Sammy shook his head. "This is NUTS!"

"That's funny," Jonathan said, holding up an M&M. "Mine are plain."

They both laughed. Then they crept once again to the edge of the roof. Jonathan carefully lowered himself.

"Hand me the rod," Jonathan instructed.

Sammy grabbed it and looped the spoons onto the hanger. Then he passed the rod to Jonathan who maneuvered the rod so that the spoons hung directly above the branches covering the Succah.

Suddenly, the moon slipped behind some clouds and the boys were enveloped in darkness.

"Hold on," Sammy whispered. "I'll get a flashlight from the box."

So involved were the two in their work that

Jonathan maneuvered the rod so that the spoons hung directly above the branches covering the Succah.

they failed to notice the group of patrol cars gathering with their lights out, on the street in front of the house.

"Now, quickly! Let's say our anthems before I fall."

In a strange mixture of Hebrew and English they each sang the anthem they knew in a whisper. As they finished, the moon reappeared.

Sammy snapped off the flashlight. "Well that's it. No problems for once. Although I still don't see what is supposed to happen. Let me just put this in the box, and I'll help you up," he whispered.

As Jonathan held onto the edge of the roof with two hands, Sammy quickly crawled back to the box. Just as he reached it a bright light and a booming sound cut through the heavy silence.

"WE HAVE YOU SURROUNDED. COME DOWN WITH YOUR HANDS UP."

"Yahhhh...!" shouted Sammy as he lost his balance and the whole box went skittering across the roof, overturning near the edge. The rope that anchored Sammy stopped him from going after it. Policemen ducked for cover as M&Ms went flying. Sammy hugged the roof trying to regain his balance.

Lt. Francis Washington stood near his patrol car, with his walkie-talkie in his hand. As M&Ms rained onto the front lawn, Lt. Washington ducked and barked into his radio, "Get us more reinforcements! And a SWAT team. I think we're onto something big!"

On the lawn, Officer Barry O'Malley ducked and rolled away from the shower of M&Ms. He didn't want to get hit by what he was sure were BBs. He shone his light on the grass. Crawling, he picked up one of the pellets.

It melted in his hands.

M&Ms? he wondered.

Back on the roof, Sammy slithered over to where Jonathan was hanging. "Pull me up. I'm starting to slip. Grab my hand." Sammy leaned over and grabbed one of Jonathan's hands. "I've got you, don't worry," Sammy assured him, as he began pulling his friend higher up onto the roof.

"WE HAVE YOU COVERED," the megaphone voice shouted, as a helicopter with a search light hovered overhead. "COME DOWN AND KEEP YOUR HANDS ABOVE YOUR HEADS."

Sammy gave a final heave and Jonathan was sprawled on the roof. Together they peered down at the scene below. Then they crawled away from the roof's edge and looked at each other. They hurriedly tried to untie themselves from the ropes.

"Well, we finished the dare," offered Jonathan, lamely.

"I wonder if your friend will send us messages in jail," Sammy lamented, raising his voice. "Because that's where we're going. As for your stupid

Zapper, they say jails are filled with bugs and mosquitoes. At least we'll have —"

Sammy was cut off as two laser beams suddenly shot into the night air probing the darkness.

"You dodo!" hissed Jonathan. "You said mosquito! You've activated the Zapper!"

"Oh no!"

As lasers probed the night, there was a frantic scurrying below. Lt. Washington ordered the recently arrived SWAT team to take up positions. "THIS IS OUR FINAL WARNING. COME DOWN WITH YOUR HANDS UP!"

Before the boys managed to reach the ladder, the Davies' front door flew open. Mr. and Mrs. Davies, and their children, Abie, Marvin and Jeremy emerged from the house in pajamas, their hands raised above their heads.

"Don't shoot! Don't shoot!" yelled Mr. Davies.

"NO, NOT YOU! GET BACK INTO THE HOUSE AND LOCK ALL DOORS AND WINDOWS!" shouted Lt. Washington through the megaphone.

The Davies scurried back into their house in a jumble. Mrs. Davies slammed the door shut, bolted it, and ordered her family down to the basement.

Meanwhile, outside, two SWAT team members were climbing up the walls of the house. Others were positioned atop neighboring houses, their rifles sending red laser beams swirling around the

Zapper. The red beams seemed small and useless compared with the constantly shifting rays of the Zapper itself. But behind those thin slivers of red light would come a barrage of bullets that could destroy the Zapper, and the boys, in seconds.

The SWAT team marksmen waited for the command to open fire.

Jonathan and Sammy carefully made their way down the ladder. Once on the ground, they faced a dozen armed policemen standing on the M&M-littered lawn. Automatic and semi-automatic rifles were trained on them.

Sammy promptly fainted.

Some people have all the luck, thought Jonathan, as he held up his hands in the glare of the spotlights.

CHAPTER 11
Primates?

The next morning Sammy and Jonathan sat eating a late breakfast in the Succah.

"I don't know about you," Sammy mumbled through a mouthful of cereal, "but I never expected to be sitting here this morning, a free man."

"To think it was Mrs. Miller who called the police!" Jonathan declared, warming his hands on a cup of hot cocoa. "Poor old Mrs. Miller. We really scared her! She looked so funny standing on the sidewalk in her striped robe and fluffy pink slippers."

"You looked pretty funny yourself, lying on the lawn in a dead faint!" Jonathan kidded. "I didn't know you could be so dramatic!"

Sammy glared at him. "And it was a good

thing I fainted, too. Otherwise Mrs. Miller wouldn't have felt so bad for calling the police. That's why she kept apologizing to us, saying how she'd thought we were burglars."

Jonathan laughed. "And the way she shooed off the cops, telling them to pretend she'd never called! 'If you *came* because I said to, then you can *leave* because I said to,'" Jonathan squeaked, trying to imitate Mrs. Miller. "She didn't even let them talk to us!"

"And you didn't even get grounded!" said Jonathan.

"Yeah. That's because you had Dad laughing so hard that he couldn't punish me!"

"I wish we had a rule like that in my house," said Jonathan as he finished his cereal. "It's great that you guys don't get punished if you can make your Dad see the funny side of the thing!"

"Really great," muttered Sammy. "Only Mom's not talking to me. Ever!" He absent-mindedly swatted a bee that was hovering near his plate. He missed.

"MOSQUITO!" shouted Jonathan, startling Sammy.

A bright beam entered through the branches that covered the Succah, and ZAP! The bee disappeared.

"Hey! It got a bee! When did you adjust it to track bees?"

"I didn't. Remember when we rigged the knob to the rope during the first dare and I moved it. Well something happened. It became stronger. Last night something else happened, and now, instead of just tracking small insects, it can track and zap bees too."

"Wow! We could get rich selling Zappers!" Sammy was counting his money already.

"But what if you were right?" Jonathan suddenly said.

"Right about what?" Sammy asked, confused.

"What if our fun-loving Goobie is not as gentle as we think?"

"What do you mean?" Sammy asked, curious as to why his friend had become so serious.

"I was just thinking. What if Goobie figures out a way — with our help — to make the Zapper zap, say, chipmunks and squirrels?"

"Well," Sammy answered, "it will be the best pest-control machine in the world."

"Maybe. But what if it's eventually beefed up enough to destroy larger things. Like primates?"

"Primates?"

"Humans, dummy. What if we are helping Goobie invent a machine that can zap humans just by saying a single word. Didn't you once mention you thought he might be dangerous?"

"Yes, but..." Sammy started to say, and then went silent.

"I think it's time for me to put a manual over-ride on this machine," Jonathan said. "Before it's too late."

CHAPTER 12
A Deed And A Dare

"Any messages?" Sammy asked matter-of-factly, as he entered Jonathan's room.

"Actually, there is," Jonathan answered, not looking up from one of his computer manuals.

Sammy stared at his friend for a moment. "Oh no! Not again! Please Jonathan, let's quit while we're ahead — and alive."

"The message is that you should call your mother when you come here. I think she wants you to babysit Abie." Jonathan started to laugh.

Sammy grabbed a pillow and threw it at him.

"And Rabbi Larry called," Jonathan added.

Rabbi Larry was the new 23-year-old assistant rabbi who was in charge of running day-to-day operations at the synagogue. He liked the kids to call him by his first name, "a warmer approach" he told their parents. The rabbi was tall and good-looking. And single.

"What's the matter, some old lady trying to marry him off again?" Sammy said.

"Not quite. He wanted to know if I could ride out to Mr. Grossman on Route 709 with a lulav and etrog. Mr. Grossman couldn't make it to synagogue this morning."

"Did you tell Rabbi Larry you'd go?"

"I told him I didn't see why not, but I wanted to make sure you could come. It'll be more fun to ride out there together."

"Right," Sammy agreed. "But if I have to babysit Abie, I may be stuck at home."

"Why don't you go home and see if you can palm him off on someone else. I'll stop by the synagogue to get the lulav and etrog from Rabbi Larry."

Jonathan walked over to get his jacket, when suddenly the Zapper came to life. Letters began to swirl around the hazy glowing mist the boys had by now gotten used to. After a minute the printer produced a paper with Goobie's familiar lettering on it.

> *BEFORE YOU GGO*
> *I HAVE A DARE YOU SHOULD KNOW*
> *MAKE SURE YOU WEAR BLACK*
> *NO COLORS SEEN IN FRONT OR BACK*

*WEAR HELMETS ALWAYS LIKE YOU DO
TO RIDE
BE READY TO RUN BE READY TO HIDE*

"Ugh! He's started rhyming again," Sammy grimaced.

"It all seems harmless enough, right Goobie?" Jonathan asked.

The printer began humming.

*AFTER YOUR VISIT BEWARE
THEY WILL STING YOU IF YOU DO NOT
TAKE CARE
FIND HORACE HE WILL MAKE IT CLEAR
TO YOU
BUT FIND HIM YOU MUST NO LATER
THAN 2*

"Harmless you said, old buddy," Sammy said patting his friend on the back. "Notice the words like beware and sting. They're almost as harmless as some of the words you use, like *trust me.*"

"He's just taking care of us, aren't you, Goobie?" Jonathan half-pleaded, looking at the steadily disappearing letters in the haze. When nothing happened, Jonathan became desperate. "Come on Goobie, don't make me do all the work. Tell Sammy it's safe. Tell him you were just kidding about beware and sting."

*I LIKE TO RHYME
SOMETIME*

"Quite a confidence builder, that last message. I certainly feel better now," Sammy said sarcastically. "All black, huh! Helmets no less! I'm surprised he didn't ask us to take swords, then we could have gone as Zorro."

"Don't worry, it'll be all right. We better get going. I'll meet you in half an hour at the old road."

"If I'm not there," Sammy told him as he walked out the door, "start without me!"

CHAPTER 13
Killer Bee Attack

Jonathan and Sammy rode in silence along the narrow, winding road. The trees, dressed in their spectacular fall colors, seemed to move apart to allow the road to pass through, then closed behind the boys as they zipped past. Aside from the occasional mailbox, there had been no sign of inhabitants for the past two miles.

Suddenly, Sammy skidded his bike to a stop. Jonathan shot past him, then backed up and pulled off to the side of the road. "What's the matter, Sam?"

"Isn't this dirt road the driveway to Mr. Grossman's place?" Sammy asked, pointing to the empty road on their right.

"Could be. I wouldn't know. I've never been to

his house before."

"I've only been here once, and my father drove that time. That's why I'm not sure."

"Maybe we should have gotten an address, or some directions beyond 'a couple of miles down the road' before we came."

"You're not getting practical in your old age, are you Jonathan?"

Jonathan smiled and started down the path. "I don't have time to be practical. That's your department."

The boys started riding again. They were so engrossed in their mission, they failed to notice the lone biker who had been following them. Now, as they made their way along the dirt path, the biker followed quietly, trying not to lose sight of them.

As they rounded a sharp curve, an old-fashioned log cabin sprang into view. Jonathan braked and stared at the house. Sammy pulled up next to him.

"This is where Mr. Grossman lives?" Jonathan asked. "In a log cabin?"

"Hey, don't knock it until you've tried it," Sammy replied. He got off of his bike and started to untie the lulav and etrog. "Mr. Grossman says he likes to live 'like people should live. Not like some hi-tech human robot.'"

"Does he have running water? And an outhouse?" Jonathan wondered out loud.

"Ask him," Sammy said as he began to tie his helmet onto the bike.

"Hey, no cheating," warned Jonathan. "Keep that helmet on."

Before Sammy could answer, a bicycle zipped around the curve. Swerving to avoid smashing into Jonathan and Sammy, the rider lost control of his bike and crashed into a tree stump.

"Ayieee!" yelled Abie Davies as he flew over the handlebar of his three-speed BMX racer.

"Abie!" Sammy and Jonathan rushed over and helped a dizzy Abie to his feet.

"What are you doing here?" demanded Sammy. "Didn't I give you five dollars to sit in front of the video until I came back?"

Abie ignored his brother and staggered over to his precious bike to check the damage.

"Are you okay, Abie?" asked Jonathan.

"I'm fine," answered Abie, straightening up. "But my bike's fender is all messed up."

"You're lucky that you're not all messed up," Sammy lectured. "You almost got brained just now, do you realize that? How would I explain a comatose brother to Mom? And where's my five dollars?"

"Forget it," Abie said. "It's going to cost at least that much to fix my bike, and since you made me swerve I —"

"What?" Sammy interrupted. "I made you

swerve? Why you — Listen, twerp, you know that Mom would never let you come out here, especially by bike. Now I have to schlep you all the way home."

"NO! I want to go where you're going," objected Abie. "I won't get in your way, I promise!"

Jonathan began walking toward the front door of the house. "Let it go, Sammy. Let's finish what we have to do so we can get on with the dare."

"Dare? What dare?" asked Abie. "And why are you guys still wearing your bike helmets?"

The older boys ignored Abie as they continued up the path to the cabin.

A wooden plaque with "Grossman" engraved in both English and Hebrew adorned the front door, and a large ceramic Mezuzah was nailed to the doorpost.

"I guess we've come to the right place," Sammy said, and knocked on the door.

After a few seconds, they heard the sound of shuffling feet approaching the door. Wearing a wool bathrobe on top of his clothing, and a scarf around his neck, Mr. Grossman opened the door. When he saw the boys, he stared for a moment and then yelled, "It's the spacemen from Mars, Regina! I think they brought the giant toothpick you ordered." Then, smiling, he let them in.

"Come on in, boys," Mrs. Grossman said. "Don't let my husband get you down. We really

*Swerving to avoid smashing into Jonathan and Sammy, the
rider lost control of his bike and crashed into a tree stump.*

appreciate your making the trip out here. But if you don't mind me asking, why are you wearing helmets?"

"It's part of a dare, Mrs. Grossman," Jonathan answered. "We have to keep them on all day."

"Pretty stupid dare, if you ask me," Mr. Grossman mumbled. "It's things like that that make me happy we're out here in the wild."

"Just ignore him, boys. Sit down." She motioned them to some wooden chairs. "Seymour, go and make the blessing on the lulav and etrog."

The boys obediently sat down in the large single room that made up the whole house. The cabin looked just as old-fashioned inside as it did outside. There were exposed wooden beams and rafters, many of them splintered and rotting, all along the ceiling. The furniture looked antique, and made the boys feel as though they were sitting in a museum. A small fire smoldered in the fireplace.

While Mr. Grossman was saying the blessings in a corner of the room, Mrs. Grossman suddenly pointed to Abie.

"Aren't you one of the Davies boys?"

"I'm Abie," he said, trying to think if he had ever met her before.

"Abie!" Mrs. Grossman exclaimed, "I can't believe how big you've gotten! I remember your Brit like it was yesterday!"

"Why does everyone say that?" Abie mumbled

under his breath.

"No one can forget your Brit, Abie!" laughed Mrs. Grossman. "The way you grabbed the mohel's beard and held on for dear life! You almost had him crying instead of the other way around!"

"Of course, he did get you in the end," Sammy said, making everyone laugh.

Mr. Grossman brought the lulav and etrog back to the table.

"I remember that Brit!" he chuckled. "It took three of us to untangle your fingers. Stubborn little baby you were! You're not like that any more, I imagine, are you?"

Abie shook his head vehemently while Sammy rolled his eyes.

"Uh, listen boys, I realize that you are on vacation, and that you took out a nice chunk of time to come here. I really appreciate that," Mr. Grossman said. "But I still think it's darn stupid to wear a helmet all day just on a dare!"

"Sure, Mr. Grossman. We're happy to have been able to help," Sammy said, choosing to ignore Seymour's remark about the helmets.

"Yeah," Abie nodded his head. "We like helping old people!"

Sammy quietly stomped on Abie's foot.

Suddenly, Mr. Grossman slapped his own neck. "Ouch!" he yelled.

Everyone looked at him. "It's those darn bees.

They're getting meaner and bigger than ever. Look," he pointed to the ground.

Sure enough there was a giant bee twirling on its side in a circle.

"Wow!" Sammy exclaimed. "That's not a bee, that's a flying horse! We could sure use the Zapper now," he said, looking at Jonathan.

"I hope you're not allergic to bee stings," Jonathan said, watching Mr. Grossman's neck swell up.

"Not me," he answered. "I used to raise bees years ago, before the wife and I retired."

"Well, just to be safe," Mrs. Grossman told him, "I'm going to put a cold pack on that."

The boys felt funny leaving, but it was close to one o'clock. Goobie had told them to find Horace by two.

"If it's okay could we leave the lulav and etrog here for a while so we can ride around a little before we head back to town?" asked Jonathan.

"Certainly," Mr. Grossman nodded, holding his neck. "There's nice land out back here, if you want to explore a little. Just be careful, there are foxes, snakes, and all sorts of creatures out there, so don't go too deep into the ravine."

"We won't go far," Jonathan assured him. "Would you know where someone named Horace lives?"

"Why sure," Mr. Grossman answered, starting

to rub his neck. "About a quarter mile down. He's got a regular house and signs posted along the way. You won't miss him."

"Thanks," the boys said in unison and rushed out the door.

Abie's eyes were opened wide. Before the door had closed behind them, he was already picturing himself battling a pack of wolves. WHACK! THWACK! SLAM! He'd defend the others. They would be stuck high up on a tree as he braved the dangers of the wilds in order to get help. No stupid little animal was going to scare *him* off, no way....

"Abie! You coming?" Sammy interrupted Abie's thoughts.

"Sure. Can you help me straighten my fender, so I can use my bike?"

Jonathan pulled out a few tools from his emergency kit and in a few minutes had repaired most of the damage.

"Good as new!" Jonathan announced, wiping his hands on his pants. "Now give me the five dollars and let's go."

"Huh? Five dollars?" Abie was confused.

"Just kidding, let's go!" Jonathan said taking off.

"Where are we going?" Abie called after Sammy and Jonathan as they headed down the driveway.

*"It's the spacemen from Mars, Regina! I think they brought
the giant toothpick you ordered."*

"Just follow and don't ask questions!" Sammy called over his shoulder.

Within minutes, the three were peddling down Route 709 in search of the signs Mr. Grossman had assured them would be there.

"There's a sign up ahead. Horace's Pottery Shed," Jonathan announced.

"And there's a private road near it," Sammy said, pointing. He checked over his shoulder to make sure Abie was keeping up with them. Sure enough, he was trailing by only a few yards.

One by one, the boys swooped onto the paved path that appeared on the left of the store.

After about five minutes, the path began sloping uphill and peddling became harder and harder. The boys tried to keep peddling, but as the incline grew steeper they had to dismount and walk their bikes. After about 15 minutes, they let their bikes drop to the ground, and sat down to catch their breath.

"Now, how are we supposed to find this Horace guy?" asked Sammy, impatiently. "I'm already wiped out!"

"Who's Horace?" Abie asked as he plopped himself on the ground.

"You'll see," answered Sammy. "We could go back to the road, but I'm sure there was a *closed* sign in the window of the pottery store. Let's leave our bikes and look around a bit. We still have some time until two."

Jonathan stood up and strained his eyes to see in the distance. To the left was a sharp slope that led into a ravine. Straight ahead led to acres of deserted wheat fields. Off to the right didn't show much promise either, with only some broken-down tool sheds visible. Weeds, vines, dried leaves and twigs littered the whole area.

"Maybe we should check one of those tool sheds," suggested Jonathan and he began picking his way through the bramble toward the nearest one.

"Hey! What about the bikes?" Sammy called after him.

"Just a second!" Jonathan called back. "Let me just go see if there is anything doing over there. If there's something worth checking out, I'll come back and we'll find some place to put the bikes."

"Look out for foxes!" shouted Abie, nervously. "And bears!"

Sammy watched as Jonathan trampled through the brittle foliage and disappeared into a shed. A few seconds later he emerged and motioned that he had found nothing, but was going to check the next shed. Abie, meanwhile, began looking around for a safe place to hide the bikes. Sammy leaned against a tree and relaxed for a few minutes.

Soon, Jonathan came tramping back with exciting news.

"One of those sheds is filled with real expensive equipment. It looks like a science lab! I wonder who hides out there?"

"It must have something to do with this fellow Horace. Goobie wouldn't tell us to find him if he wasn't around," said Sammy.

"Who's Horace? Who's Goobie?" Abie's voice startled them.

"Stop asking questions!" snapped Sammy.

Abie shrugged. "Okay! Don't bite my head off! Boy, you sure are acting weird lately," he told his older brother. "Anyway, I found someplace for our bikes. Want me to show you where?"

"Yes!" replied Sammy and Jonathan. With Abie in the lead, they made their way down into the gully. Abie directed them to a group of tall, thick bushes that formed a natural fortress around a small clearing.

"Just look out for wolves," Abie warned them as they struggled to pull their bikes into the bushes.

"And bears," Sammy reminded his little brother.

"And mountain cats," added Jonathan, just for good measure.

Abie's eyes widened in fear, and he stuck close by the older boys as they began exploring the mysterious sheds.

Suddenly, from behind them, they heard a deep-throated growl.

CHAPTER 14

The Man With No Head

"Looking for something?" boomed a hollow-sounding voice.

Sammy froze in terror. Abie's eyes were squeezed tightly shut and he was clutching his older brother's jacket. Jonathan took a deep breath and spun around.

Standing before them was the tallest man he had ever seen. At first, all Jonathan saw were two legs. When he peered nervously upwards, he could see that the man was dressed entirely in white.

Craning his neck as far back as he could, Jonathan gulped hard. The man had no head!

"My dog is not very patient," the man with no head said. "So I would appreciate an answer. What are you doing here?"

Jonathan now noticed the dog. At first he thought it was a horse, but then he realized it was a Great Dane.

At least it has a head, he thought to himself.

By now Sammy had turned around with Abie still hanging onto his pants. They both looked at the white apparition. Abie began to whimper.

Jonathan finally found his voice. "W-we were just looking around, Mister. We didn't realize this is private property."

The huge man grunted. "Actually, you look harmless enough. I just don't like people coming around bothering my beehives."

"Beehives?"

"Yes, beehives. You don't think I wear this netting on my head just for fun do you? I have eight separate hives set up just over the hill." His voice was so deep, he sounded like a bullfrog croaking.

"What do you do with all those beehives?" Sammy spluttered, while Abie stared at the dog who was just lying down, sunning himself.

"I cultivate honey, of course. But that's not the main reason I keep bees." The tall man paused and flipped up his net visor. "Do bees interest you at all?"

"Sort of." Jonathan tried not to seem too enthusiastic. Time was running out. They still had to find Goobie's Horace.

"If you'd like, you can come have a look while I tend to the last two hives, for today."

"Okay." Sammy said. Abie was still holding onto his brother as they made their way across the nearby field.

"What are your names, boys?" asked the man.

"This is Jonathan, I'm Sammy, and this is my little brother, Abie."

"I'm Horace. Pleasure to meet you boys."

"Horace!" Jonathan and Sammy exclaimed.

"Hey, that's not *such* an unusual name," Horace remarked. "Although it's probably not all that common in your generation," he conceded.

Jonathan looked down at his watch. It was almost two o'clock. That's why Goobie wanted us to get here on time, he thought. Horace must take care of his bees at two. If we had come much earlier or later we would have missed him.

The boys struggled to keep up with Horace's long strides. As they hurried behind him, Abie whispered to Jonathan, "But why is he dressed like an astronaut?"

Abie's loud whisper reached Horace's ears, and the man began to laugh loudly. The deep bellow echoed through the trees. "Like an astronaut, huh? That's a new one. Sometimes I do feel like I'm suiting up to help clear a nuclear disaster when I put on this outfit. No, it's not a space suit. It's the suit most apiarists, or beekeepers as you would say,

As they hurried behind him, Abie whispered to Jonathan, "But why is he dressed like an astronaut?"

wear to protect themselves from bee stings when working with the hives. Which is exactly what I was about to do when I noticed Jonathan peering into my work shed."

"Sorry," said Jonathan, sheepishly.

"Natural curiosity, I suppose." Horace stopped walking, and the three boys crowded around him. "There, look up ahead, do you see the hives now?"

They strained their eyes to see, then shook their heads. "I don't see anything, except for trees," answered Jonathan.

"Look closer at those trees. Can't you make out little clouds clustered around them?"

"Yeah!" shouted Sammy. "You mean that you made hives to look like trees?"

Horace chuckled. "I didn't *make* the hives, the bees did. I simply found some dying trees, and trimmed them. Then I cut a few holes in the trunk, set up my metal plates to catch the honey, and moved the hive I'd been cultivating into its new home. Sure enough, the next season the bees began to colonize another tree. Now I have eight beehives. Or at least I had eight hives."

"What do you mean *had*?" Jonathan wondered out loud.

"That's the reason I was so testy back there," Horace explained. "At first I thought poachers had come and killed the bees for their honey. But then I noticed that most of the honey was still in the trees, yet hundreds of dead bees were scattered around the area. Then the rest of the bees started behaving strangely, attacking me, and Yarborough here", he patted the dog, "without any provocation. One time I found him almost dead from the stings — he never had such a terrible reaction before. Anyway, after two hives had been wiped out I decided to do something. I travelled deep into the woods and found another hive. A monster hive."

"A monster hive?" echoed Abie, unable to control the tension in his voice.

"Killer African bees," Horace stated ominously.

"Wow! Killer bees!" Abie shouted. "Monster killer bees!"

"Anyway, I've got to check on the hives now." Noticing their helmets, he added, "You seem to be pretty well protected. Why don't you come along and watch. It's two o'clock. I've got to get home soon and make lunch for my wife. She's a first-class scientist, and a teacher. You're welcome to join us."

"Thanks," Jonathan told him. "We'd love to watch you take care of the bees but then we have to go."

Horace smiled, and added, "We're kosher, if that's what you're worried about. Anyway, we only eat health food. That's what got me started with the bees in the first place. That and the fact that I'm studying them as part of the university grant I got last year."

"How'd you know we were kosher?" Sammy asked.

"Your little brother has a kipah flapping out of the side of his helmet."

Abie, self-conscious, stuffed his kipah back under his helmet.

"Suit yourself," Horace shrugged.

"What sort of scientist are you?" Jonathan asked, wondering why Goobie had felt it was important for them to meet Horace. "I'm sort of a scientist myself."

Horace looked at Jonathan and seemed impressed.

"I'm an environmental scientist. Why don't you visit me at the university. We could talk about my project, and whatever you're working on."

"I wouldn't advise that," said Sammy. "Jonathan's projects are almost state secrets. As a matter of fact they're so secret he doesn't know what they're about, right Jonathan?"

Jonathan ignored him.

"I would really be interested in hearing your opinion about what I'm doing," Horace told Jonathan.

Jonathan couldn't tell if his new-found friend was putting him on or not. Horace had a down-to-earth honest way about him, and certainly sounded serious. Anyway, Jonathan felt he definitely needed to know what Horace was up to.

Goobie had seen to that.

They arrived in the clearing where the rotting trees stood. Horace instructed the boys to stand back while he tended the hives. He pulled down his net visor, and approached a tree. While the boys watched, he plunged his huge arms into a hollow. A few seconds later, his arms reappeared holding a large rectangular frame, dripping with honey. Bees crawled all over the frame, and a small swarm trailed after Horace as he made his way to his workshed. The boys followed at a safe distance and then peered in through a window. Horace inserted the frame into a boiling vat. After a few minutes, he withdrew the frame, left the shed and made his way back to the tree. He followed the same procedure with the second tree.

When he was done, he returned to the shed for a few minutes, then came out wearing a suit and tie, holding his beekeeper's uniform. Now that they could see his face clearly, they realized that Horace was an old man, probably in his fifties. He looked pretty regular now, except for his height.

"How tall are you, Horace?" Abie broke the silence as the group walked to a low single-storey house standing alone in the forest.

Sammy tried to stomp on his brother's foot, for the second time that day. Horace stopped him.

"No. Let him ask. Questions are healthy for a

young person's mind. I'm six-foot-ten, Abie."

"Wow! A giant!"

"Yes, that is rather tall, isn't it? I was always a head taller than all the kids in my class. Over-active pituitary gland. But nobody knew about those things when I was a kid. That's one of the reasons why I became interested in science. Hormones. I do a lot of experimenting with hormones. And bees, of all creatures, have some very interesting hormones." Horace seemed to be talking to himself at this point. "Helpful hormones. Unless those African bees come and upset the balance."

"The killer bees?" Jonathan interrupted.

Horace looked down at Jonathan. "At the rate they're moving, they could be a real problem for the *whole* continent within two years."

"What kind of problem?" asked Jonathan.

"You see," began Horace, "African bees are very aggressive. Regular bees rarely sting, and then only in self-defense. African bees, on the other hand, attack just for the fun of it. They have nasty tempers and their sting is more poisonous than your average bee's. They also attack honey bees like mine, kill them, and sometimes take over their hives. Worse still, they're dominant, so when they breed with regular bees, mostly African bees are born."

"So what's being done about the problem?" Sammy was really getting into it.

"It's a potential disaster, not only for the bee industry, but for the general population as well!" boomed Horace. "I've organized a convention of environmental experts and scientists. It starts the day after tomorrow."

"Um, Horace?" Jonathan faltered.

"Yes?"

"Would it be possible for us to attend some of the lectures at the convention?"

Horace smiled. "Certainly! I'm happy to see that you're so interested in the issue. If you come to my office at the university tomorrow, I'll give you passes so you'll be able to enter the stadium. You can also look through some of the literature I've collected about African bees while you're there."

Horace gave them specific directions to his office, then, after offering again to serve them lunch, he began walking to the house.

"Hey, where's Abie?" Sammy asked, suddenly noticing that Abie was not with them.

"He was here a minute — " Jonathan began.

"Look! Over there! What is it?" Sammy shouted. A black cloud had formed among the tall pines. The cloud was moving slowly in their direction.

CHAPTER 15
Life Saver

"That's a swarm!" shouted Horace. "A killer bee swarm. Quick, get into the shed over there. We've got to protect ourselves. Hurry! If they decide to attack us out here in the open we'll never fight them off. Run!"

Sammy refused to budge without his brother, but Horace picked him up and carried him to the safety of the shed. Jonathan was close behind.

"Don't worry about your brother," Horace said as he stuffed the boys into the closest shed. "I'll put my outfit on and look for your brother. Meanwhile, see what kind of spray you can find in here and start spraying any cracks. Don't waste time. Do it. Now."

He shut the door, put on his protective clothing, and started walking toward the swarming bees.

"What are we going to do?" Sammy asked. "I can't just leave Abie out there. What if the bees attack him?"

"You heard Horace," Jonathan told him, trying to sound calm. "He'll find Abie. We have to make sure we do as he says."

Looking around, Jonathan found some insect spray and began spraying all the cracks and crevices of the shed. He started coughing as the wind changed direction and the smell of the spray filled the shed.

"Stop Jonathan," Sammy commanded. "We'll suffocate like this."

He was looking out the small window of the shed, watching the bees as they came closer. Then, without warning, the bees raced over to where the boys were hiding, engulfing the shed in a steady "ZZZZ" that sounded like an electric saw.

"They're coming in!" shouted Jonathan, spraying again.

Bees dropped all around them, but for every bee that fell two more took its place. Part of the cloud was slowly filling the shed and the boys lashed out with anything they could find.

Only their helmets and heavy clothing prevented them from being bitten. They had put on their racing gloves and pulled down the visors of

"They're coming in!" shouted Jonathan, spraying again...But they both knew it was just a matter of time before the swarm overpowered them.

their helmets. But they both knew it was just a matter of time before the swarm overpowered them.

Then, as quickly as they had come, the bees disappeared.

Jonathan and Sammy looked at each other, stunned. Then they smelled it. Fire. Smoke from a fire outside their door was pouring in, stinging their eyes. In the haze they couldn't find the door. They began banging on the walls.

"Horace! Horace! Get us out!" yelled Sammy.

"Help! Help! Horace!" Jonathan shouted.

"What's all the shouting about?" a curious Abie asked the boys as he opened the door. He was holding a burning torch. "You guys scared me. Horace told me to hold this torch and stay near the shed while he went to get some bug spray. If I knew you guys were going to go crazy I wouldn't have done it, honest. He told me the bees were afraid of smoke and that it would scare them away. It did. But after they ran away you guys started shouting. You sounded so scary. I thought you were in trouble. Why were you hiding out in there? I couldn't find you."

Sammy was angry. "Where were you? Why did you walk away? What's the matter with you? I'm never taking you anywhere again! You hear me? Never!"

Abie had tears in his eyes. "I only did what

Horace told me to," he explained. "I had to make and I didn't want to bother anyone so I went into the woods. When I came back everyone was gone and the next thing I knew Horace told me to take this torch and go to the shed. I didn't even know where you were? Honest! I didn't mean to get you angry."

Sammy was a bit calmer now. He felt sorry for blowing up at his brother. But he was still shaking from their ordeal.

"It's okay Abie," Jonathan assured him, "we're just not used to little kids saving our lives."

"Yeah," admitted Sammy, "I'm sorry I lost it a moment ago. I just didn't understand what was happening. Thanks, Abie, thanks a lot." He hugged his younger brother.

Abie pushed away. "You mean I saved your lives?" he asked, hardly able to believe it. "I saved your lives! Wow! I'm a hero. Quick, let's tell Mom. I've got to call my friends. I can't believe it. *You both owe me your lives!* Unbelievable!"

The boys could barely contain Abie as Horace waved to them and came over.

"I see it worked. I ran to get some of this." He showed them two large containers bearing cross-bones and **Danger: Highly Toxic** signs written all over them. "But I see your brother did his job."

"Job?" Abie exclaimed. "I saved their lives! They would have been dead meat without me.

They owe me their lives. It's a debt of honor. A debt they will have to work off the rest of their lives. It's a —"

"It's a shame you won't live to see us pay off our debt," Sammy told him. "Because if you don't stop it, I will personally lock you up in that shed and throw away the key."

Abie quieted down. He knew Sammy was kidding, but with older brothers it was always better to play it safe.

"Fortunate for you boys, you had your helmets on. Which reminds me, why *do* you have your helmets on?"

"It's part of a dare," Jonathan told him.

"Well, it's a dare that probably saved your lives," Horace said, as he looked them over. "You weren't even bitten. Why don't I take you to the house and I'll drive you home. Don't worry about the bees, they won't be back for a good long while."

"I think it's better if we go back on our bikes. We left some stuff at the Grossmans."

"Well, I'll walk you back to the road, just to be sure. Once there you'll be okay."

Horace walked the boys back to their bikes and then to the road. He reminded them about the convention, and then headed back to his house.

"See," Jonathan whispered to Sammy as they prepared to get on their bikes. "I told you Goobie's dares are meant to help people. This one saved our lives, didn't it?"

"*I* saved your lives," Abie reminded him.

Jonathan ignored him. "That's why we have to go to the convention."

"You really think Goobie means for us to go to the convention?" Sammy asked.

"I'm sure of it," answered Jonathan. "What better place to demonstrate the ability of the Zapper than at a killer bee convention?"

Abie shook his head. "I don't know what you guys are talking about. Who are you going to zap? What's a convention? And when do we go home? I've got a million people to tell about saving your lives!"

Sammy looked at his watch. "Yow! It's three-thirty! We'd better get home!"

They rushed over to the Grossmans first, to collect the lulav and etrog, before racing home. Mr. Grossman was resting. It seemed the bee bite had more of an effect on him than he would have imagined.

"I think we'll go see Dr. Rothstein in town," Mrs. Grossman said, looking very worried. "Would you boys give me a hand getting Seymour into the car?"

"Sure, Mrs. Grossman," Sammy said as he and Jonathan followed her to the bedroom. Mr. Grossman's neck was swollen to twice its normal size. His eyes were glazed and he could barely walk.

They dragged him to the car. Mrs. Grossman got into the driver's seat and started the car.

"Thank you boys, I'm sure he'll be all right," she said, tears in her eyes.

"Listen, Mrs. Grossman, tell the doctor that he may have been bitten by an African bee. We just heard they're in the area. Tell him, okay?"

"Okay," she answered, barely listening. Then she drove away.

"I hope she tells the doctor," Jonathan said. "And I hope it's not true about those African bees."

"What's not true?" Sammy asked, watching the car speed away.

"That they're killers."

CHAPTER 16
The Name On The Wall

The next day Jonathan picked up Sammy and they headed for the university. Sammy kept glancing over his shoulder to make sure Abie wasn't following them this time. Once on campus they had a hard time getting their bearings.

"Do you remember where he said to go?" Sammy asked.

"Hall of Science. Sixth floor. Turn left and then straight to the end of the corridor, right turn and it's the second door after the fish tank," recited Jonathan.

"I'm glad you remember. We wouldn't even be able to ask for directions because we don't know his last name."

"You think there is more than one six-foot-ten

Horace roaming these halls?" replied Jonathan as they entered the Hall of Science building.

They found the elevators and rode up to the sixth floor. Horace's door was wide open, and the boys could hear a bullfrog voice explaining something about a microphone system to someone over the phone. When he saw the boys, Horace motioned them to come in.

Horace hung up the phone. "Glad you could make it, boys. I can't talk right now, class starts in five minutes, but I have something for you." He fumbled through one of his drawers and pulled out two passes. "Here you go, boys. The convention begins at ten o'clock tomorrow. It should be quite a learning experience. Even my wife, who hates conventions, is coming along."

Jonathan moved forward to accept the passes and thank Horace.

Sammy hung back and looked around at the different certificates on the wall. Suddenly his face turned white.

"By the way, did you hear about Seymour Grossman?" Horace asked. "African bees almost got him yesterday. Good thing someone told his wife to mention he had been bitten by one of those monsters. It saved his life. The hospital called me and I brought them some of the antidote I use in my experiments. He'll be good as new in a day or two. But it's starting. Those killers won't stop until something comes along that can destroy them. That's what the convention is all about. I hope — Hey, didn't you boys say you were at the Grossman place yesterday?"

Before Jonathan could answer, Sammy grabbed his friend's arm and started to drag him out of the office. He mumbled something to Horace while Jonathan struggled to release his arm from Sammy's tight grip. Horace smiled and waved as he answered another phone call.

"What's the matter with you?" Jonathan hissed.

"Jonathan!" Sammy whispered urgently. "Did you see the name on all those certificates?"

"What name? What are you talking about?"

"Horace the giant's last name. That's what I'm talking about."

"Horace's last name is Giant?" Jonathan asked, amazed.

"No, dummy. Horace's last name is Hensky — HENSKY! GET IT? His wife is a scientist and she teaches. She teaches at our school. Am I getting through? Horace must be Mrs. Hensky's husband!"

"Do you think so? I could never imagine her married. I figured everyone just calls her Mrs. because when you get to be her age you have to be called Mrs."

"Cut it out, Jonathan! We can't go to the convention. What if she shows up and sees us with the

Sammy hung back and looked around at the different certificates on the wall. Suddenly his face turned white.

Zapper?

"Relax, Sammy!" Jonathan said as they waited for the elevator. "Did you ever think that they may just have the same name, and not even be related!"

"Did you ever think you were insane but not yet certifiable?" Sammy countered. "Think! If weird Mrs. Hensky had a husband, wouldn't Horace fit the bill?"

"I see your point."

Sammy was getting annoyed at Jonathan's absolute calm in the face of this potential disaster. "Brilliant, Sherlock!" he said sarcastically. "Now do you agree we can't go?"

"What's the matter with you, Sammy. This is bigger than Mrs. Hensky. This is bigger than you and me. We've got a job to do. This is what Goobie has been leading us to. We can't quit now."

"Listen to yourself, Jonathan. You sound like a fanatic. God has not given us a mission. Some weird alien has given us this mission for whatever insane purpose it has in mind. We don't have to go through with this. I think you're finally flipping out!"

They entered the elevator, each avoiding the other's eyes.

Silently, they headed back to their homes.

CHAPTER 17
To Bee Or Not To Bee

Sammy and Jonathan stood in front of Gulliver Stadium. It was designed to seat 2,000 fans during the basketball season, which was about 1,800 more than ever attended any games. A giant banner hung across the front of the domed structure.

THE FIRST INTERNATIONAL
APIARISTS' CONVENTION

Jonathan had convinced Sammy to come with him, though even he had to admit he still wasn't sure what they were supposed to do, or why. His attempts to contact Goobie had proved fruitless. Then, at dawn, he had received a one-word message from the alien.

GGO!

There was a small noisy group of people picketing the convention. The protestors sported T-shirts with BE NICE TO OUR ENVIRONMENT, and SAVE THE BEES emblazoned across the front. Demonstrators were chanting, "Bee Good! Bee Beautiful! Bee! Bee! Bee!" Signs protesting bee experiments and beekeeping were everywhere. One particular slogan appeared on dozens of signs, "To Bee Or Not To Bee, That Is Our Question!". "Protect The Bees!" and "Free The Bees!" signs were also fairly popular.

Jonathan and Sammy made their way through the crowd. They tried to look casual, but being the only teenagers in the stadium made them nervous.

"What are we suppose to be doing?" Sammy whispered.

"Just look around at all the exhibits, and read as much as you can," Jonathan answered out of the corner of his mouth.

They stopped in front of a huge glass case that contained several African bees.

"Wow!" exclaimed Jonathan. "They're mean-looking! It says here that their sting is more dangerous than those of the wasp and hornet. They attack in swarms and are immune to most sprays designed to kill flying insects."

The morning was taken up with observing each exhibit and talking to several of the scientists. The boys grabbed the free literature and started reading about the plague of African bees that was sweeping north across the United States.

After a lunch break the conference began in earnest, with lectures and demonstrations by some of the over 200 scientists and researchers present. A crowd of over 1,500 — many of them townspeople — filled the stadium.

Sammy and Jonathan sat quietly. Some of the information was too technical for them to grasp, but they took detailed notes on everything that was being said.

Walking home that evening, Jonathan reviewed the day's events.

"Did you hear what that professor with the yellow bow tie was saying? About nothing being able to stop the African Bees," he said excitedly. "Honolulu! Just wait till they see what our Zapper can do! They'll never get over it!"

"That's no lie," said Sammy. "But I doubt they'll let us demonstrate our experiment. Especially since Mrs. Hensky's husband is in charge. I'm sure he knows what happened at school. And if he doesn't, the minute she sees us, he will. Lucky for us she was sitting so many rows in front of us. Otherwise you wouldn't be talking about a rematch tomorrow."

"We *have* to show it to them!" Jonathan insisted. "It's the answer they're looking for!"

Sammy shoved Jonathan onto a park bench. "Sit down, Jonathan," he began in a very serious tone. "You have to think straight for a minute. You know that if we try and rig our Zapper and something goes wrong, we'll be in big, and I mean *BIG*, trouble. No old lady in fuzzy slippers is going to save us from jail this time!"

"Who says it will go wrong?"

"Even *if* it goes right, we'll still get into trouble."

"Not if we prove that we have a solution to the problem," Jonathan argued.

Sammy shook his head. "Here's where I draw the line. You want to go, go yourself. Fourteen years old is just too young to be on the FBI's most wanted list. For all I know the Zapper may work on the bees or, as you mentioned yourself, Goobie might have souped it up so that it zaps the bee-keepers — us humans."

"I was wrong," admitted Jonathan. "I've tested and retested the Zapper. All that has happened is that it can now zap big flying insects and can do so very fast. Goobie's giving us this chance and I don't want to blow it. If you don't want to do it with me, then just help me get the Zapper to the convention. Then leave."

"That's it?" Sammy asked.

"That's it. Just help me get it there and then leave. Even though I *know* nothing will go wrong."

"And then I leave?" Sammy said again, wanting to get the ground rules straight.

"Trust me!" Jonathan smiled.

"Said the spider to the fly...or was it the bee?"

CHAPTER 18
ZAP! ZAP! ZAP!

The boys arrived at the convention bright and early the next morning. The speeches seemed to drone on and on. Jonathan's attention was elsewhere this time, as he mentally measured different points in the stadium.

At one o'clock the conference broke up for lunch, and everyone filed out of the stadium. The next symposium was called for two-thirty.

Jonathan and Sammy hung back and managed to duck behind some seats. Soon the stadium was empty.

Talking in a whisper, Jonathan outlined his plan. "...and work fast! We have to finish very quickly, because people will start coming back!"

Sammy nodded, "And once I help you get it set

up I can leave. No problem?"

"No problem," his friend confirmed.

Sammy took his knapsack and headed off to carry out Jonathan's instructions. His heart beat wildly. He wanted to get the job done and get out.

Jonathan raced up to the top row of seats, keeping a sharp eye out for any stadium personnel. He traced the metal beam he was looking for until he found where it met the bleacher stands all the way on top of the stadium. When he reached the beam he took out the Zapper and carefully balanced it on the beam. Then he leaped up and slowly began moving the Zapper across the beam. He worked quickly, wiring the Zapper to the electrical outlets that served as the power source for the main stadium lights. Then he tied the Zapper securely onto the beam.

Sammy watched from his perch at the other end of the stadium. He was lying atop the roof of the broadcasting booth. He finished wiring the fluorescent lamp and flipped the switch. It worked fine. He looked over at Jonathan for further instructions. Jonathan motioned to Sammy to meet him at the highest row of seats on the right side of the stadium.

"I'm going to rig the microphone," said Jonathan when they met. "You keep a lookout to make sure nobody's coming."

"Okay. But hurry up!"

Jonathan ran back to the broadcasting booth. The door was open and stale cigarette smoke filled his nostrils as he realized the press had made the booth their home. Luckily everyone was at lunch. He surveyed the microphones and followed the guide wires to the main panel. Quickly and silently he rigged his microphone into the panel and ran the wires out the window so that the microphone hung just above the highest entrance.

Jonathan looked down to make sure the wires had not tangled.

He froze.

Mr. and Mrs. Hensky were standing just under the microphone. It was no more than three inches above the towering Horace. Sammy stared, unable to make a sound, and remained well hidden from view.

"I think it's going well," Mr. Hensky said, as they walked down the steps towards the podium.

"I think it's going well," echoed his voice throughout the stadium.

Jonathan realized at once that the mike was on. He quickly pulled the microphone up and ducked low inside the press room.

"What was that?" Mr. Hensky asked his wife.

"I don't know," she said, looking around.

"I told those people to make sure the audio system was working properly. After this next lecture I'll give them a piece of my mind."

They both made their way down to the front of the stadium.

Jonathan lowered the microphone again, after shutting it off. This time he used a window closer to the wall of the stadium. Then he ran down, grabbed the dangling mike and found a seat in the last row. Soon people began filing back into the stadium and the next seminar was under way.

Jonathan thought he was well hidden but he kept wondering if Sammy was okay. He was also having trouble keeping an eye on the Zapper from where he was sitting.

He slowly moved into a better position.

Suddenly, Mrs. Hensky turned around and looked up. Their eyes met. Jonathan smiled weakly at his teacher. She glared back.

Like a hawk, Mrs. Hensky's eyes roamed around the stadium until she located the Zapper mounted on the high beam. Jonathan saw her whisper something to her husband, then she slipped out of her seat and made her way to the back of the stadium.

"Oh, no." Jonathan moaned to himself. "She's gonna mess everything up."

As Mrs. Hensky made her way up the bleachers, suddenly Sammy stepped out from behind a pillar.

"Hi, Mrs. Hensky!" he said brightly.

"Mr. Davies! I'm appalled at the way the two of

"I think it's going well," echoed his voice throughout
the stadium.

you have acted! Do you realize that you are endangering the lives of every person in the stadium?" She brushed past him and continued to climb the steps. Sammy followed close on her heels.

"Jonathan fixed it so it works better, now," Sammy lamely offered. "You really have nothing to worry about!"

"Nonsense," sniffed the science teacher, huffing as the climb got harder.

Just then, a commotion near the podium distracted them. Mrs. Hensky and Sammy spun around to see what was happening.

A group of protestors had pushed their way in. They were lining up on the podium, a protester behind each speaker. At an unseen signal they opened bottles of honey and poured it over the speakers. Then, one of them grabbed the microphone.

"MURDERERS!" shrieked the woman. "YOU CALLED A CONVENTION TO ARRANGE A BEE HOLOCAUST!"

Someone tried to wrestle the microphone away from her, but she continued to shout. "THOSE BEES HAVE AS MUCH RIGHT TO LIVE AS YOU DO! WHO SAYS YOU'RE MORE IMPORTANT THAN THE BEES? DO YOU GIVE HONEY? DO YOU BRING SWEETNESS INTO THE WORLD?"

Without warning, other protestors began smashing all the bee displays, including the live bee display at the far end of the hall. Then three protestors, in protective clothing, ran onto the po-dium. Each held up a bee hive. As the angry bees began swarming, the spokeswoman shouted, "NOW THE ODDS ARE EVEN. NOW THEY CAN FIGHT BACK. LET'S SEE HOW BRAVE YOU ALL ARE NOW!"

The bees began to fly around the podium as people ran for cover. Chairs were knocked over as dozens of people stampeded toward the bleachers and the exits.

Jonathan stared at the bees. They hovered for a few moments above the hall, then began regroup-ing into their characteristic swarm before they dove to attack.

The crowd bordered on hysteria as protestors, scientists, and policemen dashed for cover.

Mrs. Hensky rushed down the steps to try and help her husband take control of the situation. Sammy dashed away from her and found his way across the hall to where Jonathan was hiding.

A terrifying shriek echoed through the sta-dium. Everyone stood still.

"They're African bees!" someone shouted into the microphone. "Killer bees! Run! Run for your lives!"

Panic reigned. The escape doors were jammed with people trying to push through them.

Jonathan took a deep breath. "Ready?" he

The lasers arched out and African bees began to disappear before their eyes! Faster and faster, the Zapper spewed its deadly rays.

screamed to Sammy.

The swarms of bees hovered nearer to the fluo-rescent lamp.

"MOSQUITO!" yelled Jonathan and Sammy to-gether

Nothing happened.

Mrs. Hensky and her husband heard the boys shouting and ran over to join them.

"Louder! It's not receiving us!" shouted Jonathan. "Again! All of us!" Mrs. Hensky and her husband understood at once. They waited for Jonathan's signal.

"Now!"

"*M O S Q U I T O !*"

In the chaos Jonathan saw the Zapper beam be-gin probing the stadium.

ZAP!ZAP!ZAP!ZAP!ZAP!ZAP!ZAP!ZAP!

The lasers arched out and African bees began to disappear before their eyes! Faster and faster, the Zapper spewed its deadly rays.

ZAP!ZAP!ZAP!ZAP!ZAP!ZAP!ZAP!ZAP!ZAP!

One demonstrator raced across the stadium with a dozen African bees in hot pursuit.

ZAP!ZAP!ZAP!ZAP!ZAP!ZAP!

The woman who had interrupted the speech was screaming as a small swarm of bees made its way toward her.

ZAP!ZAP!ZAP!ZAP!ZAP!ZAP!ZAP!ZAP!

Two professors, along with a police escort,

made their way from the stadium entrance toward the bleachers where most of the demonstrators had gathered. The hovering swarm shifted and began approaching them.

ZAP!ZAP!ZAP!ZAP!ZAP!ZAP!ZAP!ZAP!ZAP! ZAP!ZAP!ZAP!ZAP!

People calmed down as they saw that the Zapper was gunning down bees at a terrific rate. The professors and policemen, even the unprotected demonstrators, began lashing out at the bees with anything they could get hold of.

A cry of victory was heard throughout the stadium as the bees began to scatter and swarms trickled down to nothing. The relentless Zapper found every bee, no matter its size, and zapped it to death.

Suddenly, without warning, the Zapper began glowing red and smoke began to pour out of it. But it continued scanning. Finally, sensing that its job was finished, its overloaded circuits just quit.

Then, while everyone was still staring at the Zapper in amazement, a holographic haze appeared just above it. Amid the "Ohs" and "Ahs" of the crowd, a jumble of letters formed itself into a single, long word.

"H O N O L U L U !"

*Amid the "OHs" and "AHs" of the crowd, a jumble of letters
formed itself into a single long word.*